BEL AIR
MAN

BEL AIR
MAN

*Teenage Sweethearts Search to Unravel
the Appearance of a Mysterious Stranger*

WARREN C. RAINER

MILL CITY PRESS, INC.

Mill City Press, Inc.
2301 Lucien Way #415
Maitland, FL 32751
407·339·4217
www.millcitypress.net

Unless otherwise indicated, Scripture quotations taken from
the New King James Version (NKJV). Copyright © 1982 by
Thomas Nelson, Inc. Used by permission. All rights reserved.

Printed in the United States of America.

ISBN-13: 9781545609781

Library of Congress Control Number: 2017952276

He liked the crunch of the snow under foot as he walked; it made his footsteps seem more important somehow, or maybe just more noticeable. The snow had fallen more than a week ago, and now it was old, mostly impregnated with dirt and frozen over from the slight warmth of the noonday sun and the hard freeze of the dark night. The short winter days seemed to collaborate with the harsh winter nights to remind the earthly inhabitants that they were not in charge of the weather, at least not yet. He didn't mind the short winter days so much, at least not nearly as much as his father, who found the truncated daylight to be a personal demon that haunted his busy workday. But for him, he liked the shorter days and change of season, and probably this festive time of year kept any longing for summer nights away from his consciousness and out of his desires, at least for now. But this time of year had its difficulties for him. Well, for someone who had only experienced seventeen earth years, they certainly seemed like difficulties.

David Edmonds knew that he had a good life, a safe and caring home, and the future seemed to be one of opportunity and options. Oftentimes he would conjure up daydreams about what he could be doing if he wasn't a teenager. During these mental sojourns, he was a mercury astronaut exploring the near reaches of space and building the foundation for future generations that would carry on to the moon, Mars, and beyond.

Reality, of course, was different. The winter months on a dairy farm in Northern Idaho could be arduous. Caring for the animals with the challenges of the cold extremes, as well as the short days, dealing with frozen watering systems, and confining them to sheltered barns, where warmth was generally determined by their ability to huddle close together near beds of clean straw—clean straw that he had to put down every Saturday morning—was hard work. The clean straw resulted from mucking out the old manure-saturated straw from the week before.

In spite of the winter chores, this time of year was always joyful for him. He loved the twinkling Christmas lights, the evergreens inside the house, and the endless array of baked goods from his mom and all the neighbors. Even the sometimes-boring Christmas pageant at school was not really so bad, though he had to play it cool with this friends and feign that he thought the play was rather lame.

Yes, today his walk on the frozen ground was pleasant, dare he say, joyful for him. He reveled in the soon-to-be-enjoyed festivities of the season. He even embraced and cherished the Christmas carols that he had heard endless times. Though he was not skilled in voice and music, he nonetheless loved to project his voice into the church enclave whenever possible. This was Christmas in Seltice Falls, Idaho. Seltice Falls was not of particular significance to anyone in the outside world. But for him and his family, actually the entire community, Seltice Falls *was* the world. A small town of 5,000 souls nestled comfortably in a narrow river valley surrounded by forested mountain peaks, this community was built around logging and mining, but there was enough of a river basin for a respectable amount of agriculture, including his parents' dairy farm. He liked to be busy and enjoyed work, so living and working on a dairy farm suited him well enough. His pleasant temperament regarding the work did not, however, translate into a desire to make milking cows his life's work; he had much grander visions for his future. These visions would vacillate from one career choice to another, but it helped keep his imagination engaged. He was actually a bit of a daydreamer when it came to his image of his inflated future self. That suited him just fine. Perhaps he was even a little proud of his ability to foster such imaginative mind exercises. After all, it was none other than Albert Einstein who used thought experiments to help visualize his most impactful theories. Being an astronaut was definitely something he thought about a lot, but such a lofty goal was tempered with a good dose of reality, even at his age. The truth was he did not really have any idea how to become an astronaut, much less any firm plans to accomplish such a feat. But for a seventeen-year-old youth in the idealistic early sixties, this did not really matter. He owned his dreams and could relish them as he wished.

It was still completely dark as he approached the milking parlor, where the cows were queuing up for their turn in the milk-extraction process. The sun had not yet dared peek over the horizon to start the day, almost as if it felt embarrassed by its inability to provide the kind of warmth that one expected from this fiery orb. His breath hung in the frozen air as he made his way to the milking parlor, the latest technology available for dairy farming. The parlor contained a pit where the person doing the milking stood, putting them below the level of the cows and at eye level with the cows' udders. This configuration allowed the person milking, the "milker," to be in a comfortable standing position rather than constantly bending over to place the milking machine on the cow's udder. It also aligned the cows' entrance and exit to the parlor in a one-way direction, which was much more efficient and less stressful on the cows, which of course helped with the overall volume production of the milk. This parlor was a modest size, six cows at a time, but it was typical for a family dairy farm. The milk was extracted using a modern vacuum system machine and was then pumped into a bulk storage tank in an adjacent room. All this equipment had to be meticulously cleaned after each use, and only special materials such as stainless steel could be used to ensure purity in the milking and bulk storage process. The parlor itself was heated to some degree by the machinery and the body heat of the cows in a confined space, so it was much more comfortable than the outside temperatures.

He pushed the door open into the bulk tank room and hung up his heavy outdoor coat. He continued on into the milking pit area to set up for the morning's chores. Once the equipment was ready, he queued up the cows into a holding area where they could enter the parlor. The cows had already worked out their own pecking order, so all he had to do was give them access to the entry door. Although cows did not strike him as very intelligent, he was always impressed at how they worked out and then honored their own social order, even for the human operation of milking them. He guessed they liked the routine and, of course, the feed bins were located at the exit to the milking parlor, which was probably reason enough for the pecking order. While he was busy getting the milking started, his dad was ahead of him getting their feed ready for the exit. His dad also took care of any unplanned actions such as sick cows, broken fences, equipment maintenance, and so forth, a never-ending task on a dairy farm. David's father, Paul Edmonds, was a down to earth pragmatic man who had a strong sense of character and a powerful work ethic. David greatly admired his father and knew that his dad had endured more hardships in life than many people would normally have to encounter. Mr. Edmonds had seen and experienced enough in World War II as a Master Sergeant in the Army in Europe to last him a lifetime. He had been with General Patton's third army as they overran Sicily and then was part of the disastrous invasion of Italy at Salerno. From Sicily all the way to Germany, he had been exposed to the worst of mankind, as well as the best. After his experiences at being part of the liberation forces of Europe, the quiet and predictable dairy life in Northern Idaho suited Paul Edmonds just fine.

Sometimes David's sister Katy came out to help if she got up in time, but generally she helped his mom with the chores in the house, and he liked that because it included the creation of a hearty breakfast once he was finished with his milking chores. Katy was fourteen years old and was capable of holding her own when it came to handling the cows and the complex milking equipment. She was competitive and a fast learner, so David sometimes had to up his game to keep up with her. His mom and dad didn't believe in gender barriers on this dairy farm. Everyone was expected to pitch in for all the chores, which meant he had to do his time at making meals and doing dishes, too. He usually started milking about 6:00 in the morning and finished about 7:30, when his dad would take over so that he could get ready for school. This worked out well for him because he was also on the high school basketball team, and he often was able to miss the evening chores due to practice, depending on how hard Coach Meyer was pushing them for the next game. He was not a great player, so he generally only got a few minutes in each game, but he enjoyed playing nonetheless. Actually he was bred with such a strong work ethic that he enjoyed practice sometimes more than the games. Playing was also a chance to show off to his girlfriend, Becky Marston.

Today was special because it was the last day before Christmas break and he would have almost two weeks without school, which was always a fun time of the year. They had a big basketball game tonight with one of their league rivals, Melton, and there was a lot of energy in the school for both the game and the break. Melton was more of a logging community and that seemed to bring out the brawn in their young men, so Melton generally dominated Seltice Falls in football. But the Seltice Falls boys usually held sway when it came to basketball. He was also thinking about Christmas break and the excitement and anticipation of gifts and of family and friends gathering for special dinners. He was old enough to know that the season was about the birth of Christ and not just about presents, but he couldn't help thinking more about what he was hoping to get for Christmas than about the two-thousand-year-old birth of a poverty-stricken baby.

He was beyond the age of wanting just "play" toys, and this year he really was hoping for something big—really big. He had been dropping hints about getting his first car. He had saved a lot of his own money, which he was more than happy to use for the purchase, but he needed not only some monetary help from his mom and dad, but their blessing as well. The latter could prove the most difficult. He had made sure that his mom and dad knew that this was all he wanted. He had daydreamed for hours about being able to drive to school in his own car, cruise Main Street, and work on the engine. This habit of daydreaming made him a victim of his own imagination regarding the exploits in the car. He dreamed up all kinds of places to go and things to do. He was sure his parents would sit back in awe once he put his mind to fixing the engine, polishing the chrome, and generally taking superb care of his first car. His desire for a car of his own was normal for a young boy of driving age, but it had become almost an obsession. He thought constantly of all the different models and types of cars that he would like to drive. He was probably partial to 1955 Chevys, but he was certainly open to anything that provided the freedom and independence of having his own car.

He felt confident that his parents would come through for him, as they usually paid attention to the Christmas wishes of their children. There was Katy, of course, but also Judy and Michael. Judy was ten and Michael was seven. Katy was working on her wardrobe, as she had grown beyond the Barbie collection, so it was not too difficult to determine what she wanted for Christmas, and the little ones got gifts suitable to their ages.

The first six cows were now in the stanchions around the pit, and he began the process of cleaning their udders and attaching the milking cups to their teats. The vacuum was already running and the machine started to milk as soon as it was attached. The milk flowed via glass piping to the bulk tank. The glass piping allowed him to see that it was flowing properly and to make sure the piping was clean after each use. There was usually a little time between the sets of six, but because different cows produced different amounts of milk, he was often going nonstop to keep up with them and the machine.

It was about seven o'clock. He was halfway through the herd with only thirty more minutes before breakfast, and man, was he hungry! As he finished hooking up another udder to the pump, another pump beeped, indicating that there was another udder signaling him for attention. As he turned toward the pump in need, he suddenly felt lightheaded and then dizzy. He saw black spots in his vision and felt like he was going to lose consciousness. He grabbed the rail beside him and steadied himself as he put his right hand to his forehead to try to balance things out. His head was now spinning and he felt disoriented. He felt a sharp pang in his stomach, and this was not for want of breakfast, and he began to feel frightened.

He closed his eyes to try to force himself back to his normal state. This seemed to help a little bit; at least with his eyes closed his mind could garner more control over this dizzy spell that was causing him to feel so disoriented. He had always been an athletic person, so he rarely experienced weakened states when he didn't feel in full control. He concentrated on bringing himself back to a steady state. He held his eyes shut for what seemed like several minutes. He did not want to risk opening them and finding that he was still not in full control of his exterior space and scope. He waited for his anxiety to settle. After what seemed a long time, he started to relax his grip on the cow stanchion rail, although he was not yet ready to open his eyes. He tried to relax his body and was actually surprised at how tense he felt. He let out a long exhale and wondered what the heck had caused the dizziness.

As he relaxed a bit, he began to feel more normal. But he noticed that the sounds that normally come with a dairy farm's milking parlor were suddenly absent. There was a surreal silence that descended upon him. He immediately thought that this had to be part of whatever was affecting his balance and again felt uneasy that he might not be in complete control of not only his senses, but his very awareness of self. As he focused on the lack of sound, he became aware of the absence of the smells that are omnipresent in a dairy parlor. Smells are the signature of a dairy, and suddenly they were gone also. With no sounds and no smells, he questioned the prudence of even opening his eyes. His mind started to race as he considered the improbability of his malfunctioning sensory input, all the while keeping his eyes tightly closed, lest he find out some reality that he would rather not confront. He centered his focus on the lack of smell, as this seemed the most foreign in the dairy parlor. He pulled larger than normal gulps of airflow into his nostrils to try to force his scent glands to find the familiar scents of the dairy barn. The large inhalations into his lungs did not improve his ability to regain the smells as he had hoped. He slowed his breathing to try to get a grip on his racing mind and make sure that he was not losing his grip on what was real here in the barn.

He finally decided he must open his eyes to bring himself back to reality and no longer depend on smells and hearing, which had obviously failed him. He gripped the stanchion bar again as he slowly opened his eyes. Somehow he was not surprised to find that the view of the parlor was there but out of focus. He pivoted his head from side to side as if searching for more friendly focus somewhere in the once-familiar but now-distorted parlor. As he did so, the milk parlor resisted him and seemed determined to stay out of focus and appear distant from his vision.

As his view rotated, he noticed a figure at the far end of the parlor. His roving eyes fixed their position on this image. Although it was not in focus, he could easily discern that this image was not part of the milk parlor's normal landscape. As he watched the figure, it slowly came into focus, even though the surrounding parlor remained blurred and out of reach. The figure was a man. He was bearded with long, tussled hair and of average height. He had a pleasant enough face, although he was not really smiling or frowning, but rather had a stoic look of strength mixed with sadness. He was dressed in a tunic and had a rough, old, worn blanket type of thing over his shoulder. His clothes were clean but worn and weathered, and they looked foreign but somehow familiar. This strange man was staring straight at him, not in a menacing way, but with a look that seemed to penetrate. As his eyes began to focus on the man, he became frightened and found himself stepping back against the side of the milking pit and gripping the stanchion rail tight once again. The strange man began to form a delicate smile, not really with his mouth but with his eyes, subtle but unmistakable. David could only stare at this man and wonder what he was experiencing here in his dad's milk barn. Who was this guy and where in the world did he come from? As much as he tried to pry his eyes away from the tunic-wearing man, he found his eyes had decided on their own to stay locked upon him for what seemed a long time.

Finally, he forced his eyes shut and shook his head to try to normalize his senses. When he opened his eyes, there was only an empty milk parlor with the smells of cows and sounds of milking machines and cows begging to be milked so that they would be allowed to get to the feed stall. In spite of his nose and ears returning to their normal duties, he remained frozen in place and continued to stare at the empty parlor space where just a moment before a strange man from a seemingly different land had stood and half smiled at him. He tried blinking his eyes and shaking his head to dislodge this experience. He felt almost desperate to somehow confirm that what had just happened had not really happened. The bellowing cows, anxious to complete their assignments, finally snapped him back to the present, and he forced himself to surrender his grip on the stanchion rail. He stood quietly in the noise and bustle of the milking parlor while he stared at the now-vacant place where the man had stood. His mind could not rationalize what had just happened. He reluctantly but dutifully resumed his milking. He began to speak to himself as if he were a counselor, assuring himself that everything was OK and that this was some kind of strange mental lapse. As a counselor he was clearly an amateur and not all that convincing.

It was raining lightly, which made the ground on the steep North Idaho hillsides dangerously slick, something that Dick Marston was accustomed to during his many years of logging the mountainous forests of this region. He wore his heavy-cleated boots to help stabilize his footing. He was the acting foreman for the logging crew under his stewardship. The contract for this part of the Kaniksu National Forest was a lucrative one for Dick and his partner, as it contained virgin Douglas fir, as well as some large yellow pine that would bring in a decent profit for their small logging business.

The crew was short-handed today due to a couple of choker setters being sick, or at least that's what they said. Dick knew these two and suspected that they had spent too much time at the local tavern the night before. The choker setter's job is to wrap freshly cut fallen logs with choker cables. The cables tighten as tension is applied, choking the log, if you will. Once captured in this way, the log can be dragged via an overhead cable line or via bulldozer to a staging area, known as the log deck. Setting choker cables can be dangerous work, especially on steep, wet ground. Fortunately for Dick, he had Bobby Bresberg there today. Bobby was young, full of vigor, and could do the work of two men, if needed. Although Dick was fifteen years his senior, he and Bobby had become good friends, on and off the job.

Dick was the kind of boss that stepped in whenever and wherever needed, so today, being short-handed, he was in among the fallen timber, setting the chokers, while Bobby ran the bulldozer winch to get the prized logs to the log deck. Dick was pleased with the harvest from this south-facing hillside—large, knotless Douglas fir that would bring a premium price at the sawmill.

Dick was panting as he raced, slipped, and staggered from log to log to try to keep pace with Bobby and get the timber to the log deck as quickly as possible. Haste was not to be Dick's friend today, as he did not see the deadly kink and associated fray in the cable as he cinched up yet another promising fir log. Compounding his haste was the mud clinging to the cable, perfectly disguising the fray so that it appeared to be an otherwise trustworthy cable.

Bobby applied power to the winch and the cable slack snapped tight, quickly compressing around the waiting log with deadly force. The log jumped to life as it began to traverse up the hill. Logging a hillside is always done top to bottom to minimize workers being in the path of an errant runaway timber log, machine, or anything else that might be loose on the hillside. Dick made sure he had stepped a safe distance away from the log as it slithered upward, and he kept his eye on the log, cable, and Bobby as the log progressed.

Dick's keen eye scanned up the cable and stopped suddenly as he observed what a choker setter never wants to see, the fray in a damaged cable! Just as he was raising his arm to signal Bobby to stop the powerful winch, the over-stretched cable sustained a massive failure. As if in slow motion, the individual strands of braid that make up the usually reliable cable began to sever one by one in rapid succession, and the cable began to stretch as the momentum of the logs slowed in concert with each snapping braid. Dick's watchful eyes widened as he realized what was about to happen as the cable would soon separate and snap back with such force as to cut a man in half.

The last seconds of Dick Marston's life would be ever frozen in Bobby Bresbergs mind. The wildly slashing cable moving with such speed and force that it was almost mesmerizing. For Bobby, the sickening slash of the cable into Dick Marston's head was something he would relive for many sleepless nights afterward. No matter how fast Bobby dismounted the bulldozer to race to Dick's side, he already knew the outcome. There was no possible scenario in which a man could survive such a blow.

December 21, 1962 — 7:12 a.m.

Becky Marston liked life in Seltice Falls. The beautiful mountain backdrop of the valley was a canvas where the seasons of the year could paint their colorful majesty in a never-ending and somehow never monotonous cycle of color, environments, wonder, and experiences. Becky lived with her mom, her brother, and her little sister. Her brother, Roger, was a senior in high school, which, to a sixteen-year-old, was a grown man. Probably in her brother's case, the grown man mantel fit well, as he had been the man in the family since her dad was killed in a tragic logging accident three years ago. The day of the accident had been the worst thing that Becky had ever experienced. Even today, with three years between her and this tragedy, the pain and sorrow was still acute and still almost numbing. No matter how she tried to move beyond it, she never could escape it. It seemed like a hidden beast that would make uninvited intrusions into her psyche on a daily basis and put darkness on her heart that always took time to dissolve.

Her little sister, Junie, was very small at the time of the accident so was not so aware of the impact on the rest of the family. Junie was a bouncing ball of energy and always seemed to press the norms of behavior, oftentimes to the frustration and outright anger of Becky, who was quiet and reserved, and not one to make a scene or want to be in trouble for anything. Junie was really not so bad; Becky knew this. She was just too full of energy for such a young body to contain.

Becky's mom had suffered through the loss of her life's partner with grace but not without pain and agonizing grief. Mary Marston had made herself into a pillar of strength after her husband's death. She knew that this is what you did to carry on and make sure the family could survive. Fortunately, Dick Marston had a life insurance policy, which allowed Mary to carry on raising the family as best she could without her partner. Mary had also taken on outside work as a receptionist and administrative assistant for the local law office of Ogden and Schultz. This put a squeeze on raising the family, but it provided a much-needed financial boost, as well as a psychological one for Mary. The work gave her an outlet from her grief and provided her a busy schedule, which proved to be a welcome elixir for dealing with the loss of her beloved.

Becky was anxious for Christmas like most of the young people in Seltice Falls and around the world. She liked the festive time of year, and with the loss of her dad, it was a time to reconnect with members of her dad's family. In this way she could feel as if she were with him again. Her uncle Dan's laugh and his mannerisms were so similar to her own dad that she could almost feel a spiritual connection with her dad just by visiting with Uncle Dan. Uncle Dan had also been there for them after the accident, so Becky felt a special connection to him. Dan lived about two hours south on Highway 95, so she did not get to see him as much as she would like, but at Christmas the family always got together, and Becky loved it.

Becky was a student who always made honor roll but was not the "straight A" type. She probably let herself get a little too distracted with life to get to that level. She did like school, however, because she had a lot of friends and enjoyed spending time with them. She was active in church activities as well and enjoyed the projects and pageants that were part of it. She was in the church choir, which was special, as most of the choir was older, but she had a gifted voice and truly loved singing the hymns at church. This made Christmas special because she loved all the carols they got to sing this time of year.

Becky loved the festive parts of the holiday as well, and she had her heart set on some special gifts for Christmas. She knew well that her mom was always challenged financially, but in spite of this she always came through to make this time of year special. This year she was hoping for mostly new clothes, as she had made the transition from the toys and dolls of her youth. She also loved to get new games. She enjoyed spending time with her friends on a sleepover or even with her family playing the latest games. She really liked Parcheesi, and she was quite skilled at it. She liked it because on the surface it appears to be a simple game but to a skilled player like her, there was a lot of strategy to use against your opponents. Becky's brother, Roger, refused to play with her anymore as he was frustrated with her winning streak, but what he really hated was her superior skill at the game. Roger was a good athlete and was very competitive so he did not take kindly to losing to his baby sister.

Athletics had been Roger's lifeboat when their father was killed. He found that the stress and strain of aggressive workouts and practice was the elixir he needed most for his grief. Roger had been close to his father, and his dad was his hero. The loss was almost more than he could bear. Football had really been his main outlet; the raw aggression and physical contact gave Roger a way to stave off or at least ignore his emotional pain. Roger had been thrust into a role he did not want when his dad died. He suddenly was the man of the house and, as such, had to skip over some of the years of his youth on his way to adulthood. He had managed it well enough, and although there were many missteps, he had risen to the challenge. He had insisted on quitting sports to help his mom, but his mom would have none of it and made sure he kept to his sports regimen.

Becky's family lived in a modest but charming home in Seltice Falls. It was a bungalow style built in the 1930s and had been well cared for. They lived in a pleasant neighborhood; frankly, in Seltice Falls there were really few unpleasant ones, and Becky enjoyed being within walking distance to her friends, school, and shopping. In fact, she was planning on walking to the big basketball game tonight against Melton. It was a home game and she was looking forward to seeing all her friends before Christmas break. She also wanted a chance to see David Edmonds play and see him after the game, even if for only a few minutes. She and David had become sweet on each other, although up to now their relationship was not overly serious. David did too much thinking about the future for that, but they did like each other, had spent a lot of time together, and had been out on several official and many not-so-official dates. David would visit at the Marston home and could always lighten Becky's spirits, no matter what the day had wrought. Becky felt secure and content when she was with him and found him to be more of a gentleman and, at least to her, more worldly than other guys in her grade. He liked to tell her about his dreams about the future. Becky enjoyed this time together. She also thought about the future but not in the futuristic way that David did; to her it was more about escaping Seltice Falls and seeing faraway lands and people, and exploring the great cities of Europe and mysterious Asia. This distinction seemed to have a polar opposite attraction effect upon them and enhanced their time together. Becky and David had kissed and made out but nothing more adventuresome at this point. Right now their "love" was as modest as young sweethearts could be, and David had no idea what to do with it or about it. In the end, it was a perfect high school romance, puppy love by any other name.

Mary Marston was shouting to everyone to come to the breakfast table and get their morning meal before they all had to go their separate ways for the day. Becky and Roger hurried to the table, as they both had eager appetites to satisfy. Mary put on a training table breakfast for someone with so little free time and so many responsibilities—a pot of oatmeal, followed by fried eggs, bacon, and some toast—all with smells that would waft through the house and torture anyone who was not at the table. They all made small talk. Roger had to give Becky some ribbing about hooking up with that "Edmonds" kid at the basketball game, and Becky gave it back to him about his own attempts at early romance, which for Roger had not been very fruitful. Roger's unexpected and reluctant admission to an early adulthood had made it difficult for him to connect with many of his classmates, so he tended to be a bit of a loner, except for his sports teammates. Through their shared tragedy, Roger and Becky had become close comrades in supporting their mom and each other whenever a dark day would engulf them. They did like to kid with each other, but it was always with the love they shared.

Once breakfast was completed, they all pitched in to assist with cleaning up the dishes, countertops, and left-overs. They had a well-practiced routine so that everyone took their part and things got finished quickly and efficiently. Once the kitchen duty was complete, Becky finished preparing for school, dressing and putting on enough makeup to look older than her sixteen years but not so much as to gain the ire of her mom about looking "trashy." She had this practiced to an art but just in case would carry enough supplies in her purse to do any touch-up at school that might be required. This was also kind of a ritual, as most of the girls in her class would be in the girl's bathroom before school started adding that tiny bit of extra eye-liner. Once all was in order, she grabbed her lunch bag and schoolbooks and, with a quick kiss to her mom, was suited up for the cold walk to school. At least the sidewalks had been cleared so she did not have to walk over ridges of refrozen snow and ice. Seltice Falls was a small town, so she could walk to school in only about fifteen minutes, but she was certainly ready for some indoor heat by the time she arrived.

She went through her eyeliner touch-up, chatted with her friends, and then started looking around the halls for David Edmonds. The dairy farm was too far from school to make it walkable, so he was stuck riding the bus. She was glad to be spared that torture. The buses usually arrived early, so he was generally at school before she was. While it was customary to walk the halls of the school with your friends or your sweetie, if you had one, Becky and David did not walk the halls together; they had not really discussed it but they both sensed that they were not really that intertwined yet, and so they kept their interactions a bit more discreet. Nonetheless, she found David by his locker speaking to Mike Glatter, one of David's closest friends. It seemed they were having a rather dark conversation, so Becky pretended not to notice and started to walk away, but Mike called out to her.

"Hey, Becky, you better see if you can cheer this guy up." Becky stopped and turned to face them, feeling a bit awkward, as she did not know what Mike was referring to. Becky approached them with a smile in an attempt to make light of whatever situation was brewing between the boys. When she looked at David, she saw a troubled look on his face and not the usual upbeat *I am going to conquer the world* expression that she was used to seeing.

"David, are you feeling OK?" she said, as she tried to make eye contact with him.

"Yeah, I'm fine. Mike is making a big deal out of nothing," David responded quickly but kept his eyes downcast.

"He had some kind of weird dizzy spell this morning and lost his vision and, what did you say, your hearing, too?" Mike said.

"What? That doesn't sound normal at all. When did this happen? Did you fall or something?" Becky could not hide the look of concern on her face.

"Look, it's nothing. I think I probably just got light-headed this morning while I was milking the stupid cows. I'm sure it's nothing." David was not very convincing, and Becky was sure there was more to this story than he was providing.

"Are you feeling OK now? Are you still dizzy and can you see OK?" Becky was not going to let it go that easily.

"Oh, for Pete's sake, it's nothing, you guys need to drop it . . . OK?" David was now a bit irritated.

"It's not nothing. People don't just lose their vision and hearing for no reason. You need to make sure your mom knows what happened, and maybe you shouldn't play in the game tonight?" Becky was now standing very close and trying to look into his eyes.

"All right, I'm going to class now and, yes, of course I'm going to play in tonight's game! Now can we please drop this?" David grabbed his books and headed for his class, clearly irritated with the conversation.

Becky gave Mike a look of bewilderment, shook her head, and started off for her first class. Mike shrugged his shoulders and also went on his way.

Chapter 3

The team sat in a semicircle in the locker room just before warm-ups, while Coach Meyer gave them some last-minute instructions, mixed with some inspirations and tired, old sports metaphors. Mike was sitting opposite the semicircle from David and was watching him closely to see if there might be some hint of things being not quite right. Being a starter, Mike should have been listening to the instructions from Coach Meyer, but he could not help but keep his eyes on David. There was nothing obviously different about him, except that the normally energetic Mr. Can-Do attitude he had was clearly absent. Mike also felt that David had not told him the whole story and wondered what had really happened to his friend that morning.

The team broke the session and entered the gym among the hoots and hollers that the home team usually enjoys. They went through their warm-up routines; the starters wore their game-ready uniforms while everyone else wore the outer warm-up garments. Mike kept glancing at David to see if he seemed OK as they went through the familiar drills. Although David's behavior was not different enough to draw notice from anyone else, it was clear to Mike that his mind was definitely distracted. The normally rah-rah Mr. Edmonds was more mechanical than fluid in his motions and drills.

Almost midway through the game, the score remained close, although Mike seemed to be shooting cold tonight. He had missed a layup earlier that made him feel more foolish than anything else. He usually made a decent jump shot, but tonight it seemed he could only shoot up bricks. Coach had taken him out and told him to take a breather and relax. David had not gotten into the game yet, but he seemed to have come out of his trance a bit after the warm-ups and the game had started. Mike always thought David was a bit strange the way he enjoyed practice, and even the whistle drills, for heaven's sake. Who in their right mind enjoyed whistle drills? Mike could only shake his head.

Becky was sitting with her friends, and they were all enjoying the close game. Because it was a home game, they tried to make as much noise as possible. It was only a high school game, but in a small town, that was equal to the Steelers in Pittsburgh. With Christmas break upon them, the atmosphere was electric and fun. Becky kept her eye on David and he seemed quite normal, so she started to relax about her earlier concerns regarding his episode that morning. So far David had spent the night on the bench, so there was not much to observe.

With five minutes left in the first half, Coach Meyer looked down the bench and barked at David, "Edmonds, get in there for Johnson. Give him a breather. He keeps letting that guard drive the lane. Let's get a stop in there, OK?"

Of course, David jumped up as if on a spring, excited to be going in as a solution instead of a filler at the end of the game. Johnson was usually a decent guard for passing and shooting, but he was struggling guarding the lane to the basket, and the kid from Melton was quick with the head fake and found he could twist around Johnson for that sweet drive down the lane. David gave Johnson a hand slap on the way into the game, and he could hear Mike shouting behind him, "C'mon, David, nail these guys!"

David's energy had been attenuated during the day from his experience in the morning, although he was not really aware of it as it had been subtle and in his subconscious. Going into the game released him from this cloud, and he felt a burst of energy and confidence that was foreign to him. He literally bounded onto the hardwood amid pats on the back from his teammates. David eagerly took the inbound pass from Jimmie Koffler and dribbled down the floor to set up the play formation. As he watched the speedy guard from Melton angle to cover Koffler, the lane through the paint seemed to open before him. He was not normally inclined to make such a drive to the basket but this infusion of energy from an unknown source propelled him into the key and to the hoop. Melton's center was caught completely off guard as this second stringer fresh off the bench suddenly streaked by him and put in a beautiful layup off the glass.

Becky squealed with delight as she watched David drive fearlessly and with undeniable and unfamiliar skill to the hoop for a basket. She grabbed her friend Patty's arm and squeezed it as she cheered. Patty laughed at Becky's reaction.

"Becky, calm down, it's just one basket, for heaven's sake. But, oh yeah, I forgot it's your sweetie."

Becky didn't mind the reference to David as her sweetie. It made her giggle even more and bounce on the hard bleacher seats. The Melton offense was quickly back up the floor now, leading by eight points instead of the magic ten, thanks to David's bucket.

Just as the left guard tried a bounce pass inside to the center, David sprung like a cat and, injecting his hand into the ball's errant trajectory, snatched the pass in mid-bounce.

24

He even surprised himself. As his reverse momentum carried him and the ball away from the forward motion of the opponent's play, he found himself alone as he drove the length of the gym floor and bounced another seemingly perfect layup off the glass backboard and swished the net cleanly. The hometown crowd erupted in cheers, hoots, and unfamiliar adoration for this unknown second stringer. Coach Meyer was standing jubilantly with his arms raised in a victory pose, while his mind was trying to understand who put the voltage into the Edmonds kid. Dick Meyers was a young coach, but this was *his* team and he loved it. Dick grew up in the suburbs of Seattle, but after his own basketball career came to an unceremonious conclusion at the end of college at Whitworth University in Spokane, he found success teaching and coaching various sports teams. He had bigger dreams than Seltice Falls, but right now for him there was no other place he wanted to be and coach. After Seattle he thought he would hate such a small town, but it had actually grown on him. And though he missed the amenities that Seattle had to offer, he loved the notoriety that being "Coach" in a small community brought him. He had also been surprised how well he adapted to the rural lifestyle and friendly people. He had coached enough that he felt he could gauge players' skills well enough to find the best way to win games. This unexpected flurry from David Edmonds, however, was new to him, and he was enjoying the puzzled delight of this unpredictable moment of glory. He hoped that somehow this was tied to his coaching. He thought to himself that this *must* be due to his coaching.

The Melton players were a bit stunned. There was no question that David had suddenly electrified not only the gym crowd, but also his equally surprised teammates.

Becky was now on her feet with all of her friends, but all she could do was giggle with delight. She was not so passionate about beating Melton, but to see David be the star was magic to her. Her energy was infectious to her friends as well, and they all stood and boomed their audio waves of approval.

Although Melton's offense still held the lead on the scoreboard, they had taken on the demeanor of defeat as they worked the ball back up the court. The Melton guards weaved the ball over the half court and cautiously avoided David Edmonds as they dribbled and passed the offense back up the floor. David was not impacted by the quick realignment of the offense as it related to him; he pressed every move by the left guard as the Seltice team stayed in their man-to-man defensive formation. The right guard called the play for Melton, as the team slowed into position to work for an open shot. Melton wisely used their play setup to work their positions, but the Seltice defense, mostly inspired by David's energy, would not yield the shot that Melton desired.

The right guard could not press the relentless defense any farther and recklessly attempted to drive the lane. The guard was quick and found enough space to make it into the top of the key, but the impatient effort did not get him in the position he wanted for a layup shot, and the ball skidded too hard off the glass backboard and bounded straight away from the stubborn rim. As the ball raced toward the center of the key, David spun from his position on the left flank and propelled himself skyward to literally rip the escaping ball midflight. As gravity returned his feet to the hardwood, David flayed his elbows to ensure a clean rebound without a possession whistle. As David gave a quick look down court, he could see his fellow guard, Robbie Preston, racing away from him. David was usually more of a cerebral player and played more with his head than his heart, which oftentimes cost him precious microseconds to hit an opportunity. This time was different though, as he sensed the moment instinctively and he accurately lobbed a court-long pass to Robbie as Robbie was breaking into the open and driving to the basket. Robbie followed through with a layup.

The energy in the gym was now contagious, not just for the spectators but for the players as well. David's inspirational play was infectious, and everyone was fueled by it. With only seconds left in the half, the Melton coach quickly called a time-out before they could inbound the ball again. Melton's coach knew he needed to find a way to slow down the electricity that was clearly energizing Seltice's team. On the Seltice bench, Coach Meyers tried to give an inspirational chat to his team, but he found that he struggled to find the right words to fit this unusual circumstance, so he closed by praising David's play, as the other players nodded their acknowledgment. But their gazes toward David communicated more puzzlement than inspiration.

The halftime came with the score tied, but the atmosphere in the gym felt much more one-sided than the scoreboard could acknowledge.

As Coach Meyers spent the time trying to leverage his sudden and unexpected coaching success, Becky and her friends were all grabbing some peanuts and popcorn and chatting excitedly about David's play and the quick turn of momentum they just witnessed. Becky made eye contact with David's father and gave a quick smile and nod, which he acknowledged and returned. Becky and David's father did not really know each other except by small town acquaintance, so this acknowledgment by him of her even existing put helium into Becky's step, as she and her group made their way back into the gym and their seats.

No one except David was surprised that he was going to start the second half, something that he had only done when the normal starters were unavailable. This time it was because he was the better man on the floor. Coach Meyer was smart enough to play a good hand when he held one, even if he wasn't sure how it was dealt to him. David's high-energy play continued as they started the second half. He hit a swish perimeter shot to give Seltice the lead and give Melton's coach a quick twist of the gut. Melton started double-teaming David, but they were not skilled enough to spread their defense across the floor and that left too many Seltice players with open shots. Before the second half had everyone back in their seats with fresh popcorn, the Seltice boys had pushed the lead to ten points.

Melton tried to slow the pace with a quick time-out, but their next drive resulted in another poorly positioned shot. As David sent the inbound pass to Robbie and started up the floor, he gave a quick look into the busy bleachers to make sure Becky was absorbing his newfound stardom. As his eyes scanned quickly to pick her face from the crowd, he found something he did not want to see. It was the same man from the dairy parlor seated in the top row of the bleacher seats. This froze David in his tracks. The shock of this troubling vision caused David's stride to buckle underneath him, and he tripped on his own forward motion. As he pitched forward on the hardwood, he caught himself with his hands while maintaining his locked vision on the man with the old tunic, beard, and long hair. He ended up on all fours as the crowd let out a collective gasp, partly from their shock of seeing this newfound star stumble and partly from the sound of David's skin burn as he skidded on the oak hardwood. David stayed frozen in place on his hands and knees while staring at the top row of the bleachers, straight into the eyes of this strange man. He couldn't understand what in the world he was doing at the game. He noticed that his senses had once again taken leave of his person and his total focus was this top-row tormentor. The man returned

David's stare and once again had a subtle smile. As David watched, the man shook his head slightly from side-to-side indicating a soft no, the kind of no that transfers guilt or says, "you know better." David was transfixed and lost all sense of time and place.

The loss of his senses was now not confined to hearing and smell but also to his nervous system. He had no sensation of the floor burns that were solidly affixed to his knees. He had a floating sensation and felt like he was in a type of trance that seemed to be transmitted through the eyes of this man. The man continued this condescending stare and slight side-to-side shake of his head, implicating some kind of disappointment. As David focused on the man, he realized that everything and everyone in the gym was out of focus. His vision was just a single funnel focused on the tunic-clad tormentor in the stands. David dug deep into his psyche and pulled up enough determination to study and analyze the figure. The man actually had a pleasant enough face, although one that was worn, not so much from age but from a life lived with hardship. It was also a face that looked to contain a discernable amount of wisdom. The beard and long hair were tended but still had an unkempt look, and David was not sure he could describe it if asked. The tunic garment appeared to be heavy wool and roughly made but had a distinct quality, a homemade look but appeared very durable. The man looked like he was from another era and certainly not someone who should be in Seltice Falls at a basketball game.

"Time!" bellowed Coach Meyer as he scrambled from the bench toward David. David's collapse was so odd that the coach did not even wait until Robbie made his way down the floor to set up the offense for the next play.

The coach knew better than to put a hand on David right away because he didn't really know if he was injured.

Instead, he stopped right alongside him and got down on one knee where he could level his gaze even with David's head height, as David remained on his hands and knees. As the coach said David's name, he noticed immediately that David was staring at the upper bleachers. His stare was so locked into place that the coach initially had the panicky thought that he may have a head injury or worse. Coach Meyer knew that aneurisms in high school athletes were not unheard of, and they were often fatal.

The coach looked quickly up into the empty top row bleachers and then back at David, only to find David's stare unchanged. "David!" shouted Coach Meyer as he snapped his fingers in front of David's eyes. The trance broke, and David suddenly exhaled and started shaking violently as he collapsed onto the gym floor. David's quick reaction caught the coach by surprise and he jumped back as David crumpled.

David recovered quickly and to his embarrassment found himself face-to-face with Coach Meyer in the middle of a gym that was suddenly as silent as the grave. "David, are you all right, son?" Coach Meyer said, as he recovered from his start at David's collapse.

"David, look at me, right here." Coach Meyer was now using his take-charge voice as his anxiety over the unknown dissipated. The coach grabbed David's shoulder as David sat up on the floor and once again looked for Becky in the anxiety-riddled faces in the bleachers. It took David a couple of seconds to find Becky's face staring straight at him from halfway up the bleachers, actually not too far below where that man was sitting. David turned his attention quickly to where the man was sitting and saw he was no longer there. He looked around but saw no sign of him anywhere in the bleachers.

David suddenly stood up and literally started to turn in a 360-degree arc, looking around the gym for the man. There was no way he could have gotten out of the gym that fast. David looked fearful and anxious as he scanned every space of the gym as quickly as his eyes could manage.

Coach Meyer now grabbed David by the shoulders. "David, David, what are you looking for? Are you all right? You shouldn't have gotten up so fast. C'mon, son, let's get you into the locker room and make sure you're OK."

"Coach, I need to look for him. I can't go to the locker room yet. I'm fine." David protested.

"Look for who?" Coach was really wondering now what was going on with this kid.

Coach's question bit into David's mind and made him realize what he hadn't even remotely considered, that he was the only one seeing this guy! It hit David that this was only in his mind and not something that was going on with everyone else. He had no way of understanding anything else, but this much he knew—he needed to play it down or everyone was going to think he was losing it. "I'm fine, Coach. I'm OK. I must have just gotten dizzy or something like that."

As Coach absorbed this feeble reasoning and continued to stare into David's eyes, he tried to decide if this kid was really OK or if there was something more sinister going on. "Well, we can't take any chances, David. I want you to go into the locker room with Coach Rackney and the trainer to make sure you're all right."

After being monitored through most of the second half by the trainer and assistant coach Rackney, David returned to the bench with a couple of minutes left in the game. Even his dad had come into the locker room to check on him, which he expected, but it was embarrassing nonetheless. David did not share with anyone what he had really experienced. He felt he had to figure it out himself before consulting with the adults. He knew instinctively that they would probably overreact.

Melton found energy in the demise of David's short star career and slowly climbed back into the lead. They were able to leave the gym that night victorious. After David's strange experience, he was only able to muster a weak interest in the outcome. It was not that he didn't root for his team, but he had a deeper foreboding concern about why he was having these hallucinations or visions.

"David, come see me in my office when you're finished showering and dressing," Coach Meyer said, as David weakly went through the mechanical motions of morphing from basketball star to awkward teenager. In somewhat of a daze, David finished dressing and made his way to see Coach Meyer. He had a dark cloud shadowing his every step as he approached the office. He wondered how he was going to explain his strange behavior and mishap during the game and his short burst of athleticism that put Seltice Falls in the lead for the better part of the second half. He didn't have any idea what was going on in his life with this strange guy who seemed to be appearing at random and why this weirdo was only visible to him. Who was this guy and why was he tormenting David? David stopped for a moment a few steps from Coach Meyer's office to try to think about what he was going to say. He decided not on what he *would* say but on what he *would not* say. He was not going to tell him about this man appearing in the bleachers, at least not yet.

"So, David, have a seat there by the desk," directed Coach Meyer as he pointed lazily to the tired, old desk chair that had once been the center of Mrs. Galich's algebra class but over the years had found its way to various lower levels of use and was now unceremoniously the visitor chair in Coach Meyer's office. David sat down lightly on the edge of the chair, feeling nervous and uncomfortable. It occurred to him that he had never really had this type of one-on-one chat with his coach, and he certainly did not feel like breaking his streak and starting a chat now. He especially did not want to share an honest report of what had happened tonight.

"David, what exactly happened out there tonight? Is everything OK? I mean you played great tonight but then you seemed like you really had some kind of . . . of . . . a seizure or something? Look, son, I just want to make sure you are OK. Are you OK?" Coach asked.

"Yeah, sorry, Coach, I guess I was kind of a spaz out there tonight. I don't really know what happened when I fell down. I guess I kind of got dizzy and lost my balance or something." David offered but not convincingly.

"Well, David, a dizzy spell can be something more serious, you know. I'm going to insist that your parents get you checked out with Dr. Broman, OK? And what was it you were staring at in the bleachers? I didn't see anything where you were looking." Coach Meyer quizzed as he lowered his gaze directly into David's eyes.

"Gosh, Coach, I guess, well, I guess that maybe the dizzy spell just caused me to look there and try to get my bearings. Yes, I think that was it. I was trying to get my bearings." David realized that this quickly and randomly conjured-up explanation actually sounded pretty good. In fact, it seemed so plausible that he started to think that maybe that was really what had happened and there was no strange man haunting him after all. "Yes, Coach, I think staring at the bleachers helped get me grounded again and dissipated the dizziness."

The coach leveled his eyes at David and studied him for a few seconds, which seemed an eternity to David. He realized he was sweating under the coach's menacing eye-balls and wanted to shout, "What? That last answer was pretty darn good, so what are you looking at anyway?" But, of course, he just squirmed nervously in the old desk chair without saying anything to the coach.

After a lengthy silence, the coach got up and repeated to David that he wanted him to make sure his parents got him checked by Dr. Broman as soon as possible. He patted David on the back, congratulated him on his great playing, and said he hoped he would see that kind of performance again in the future. David thanked Coach and assured him that he would do his best for the team, and then got out of the office as quickly as possible. He grabbed his winter coat from his locker and headed for the exit.

His parents were waiting for him in the car, with the motor running to keep out the cold, which was what they always did after a game. As he started toward the car, he heard a familiar voice call out.

"David, David, can we talk for a minute." It was Becky. She had been waiting for him along the side of the gym building. "I was so worried about you when you fell and had to leave the game. Are you all right?"

"Becky, you shouldn't be waiting out here in the cold like this. What are you doing?" David responded.

"I'm worried about you, you knucklehead, what do you think? What happened in there anyway? Gosh, the way you fell down and then just looked off into space. David, I was really worried." Becky's eyes were locked onto David's and were moist with tears. "Did you have another loss of vision or something?"

"Of course I didn't have a loss of vision. I just, you know, I just got dizzy and fell down, that's all." David's response was defensive and too quick to really be very convincing. Becky's female intuition was strong, and she was not so easily dissuaded.

"You had another hearing and vision issue, didn't you? Was it the same as this morning in the barn? It was, wasn't it?" Becky was not to be rebuked.

"It was nothing, Becky, really. I'm fine. Look, I appreciate your concern but it's nothing, I just got dizzy, that's all." David offered.

"David, you're not very good at lying. I don't know what happened out there tonight, but it wasn't just being dizzy. Being dizzy does not look like that and you know it. Are you going to tell me or should I just make something up to tell all my friends?" Becky had a slight smirk with this comment because she would not really torture David with that kind of gossip.

"Dang it, Becky. Please don't tell that gang of yakkers you hang out with it. I'll be the idiot of the school," David quickly responded.

"Oh, you know I won't, but you're going to have to tell me the truth sooner or later and you know it," Becky offered firmly but kindly.

David looked this girl in the eye now. "Ok, Becky, but let me think about this a bit. I'm not sure myself what is happening. OK?"

"Well, we'll see, but don't let this continue without telling someone, got it?" Becky held his gaze.

David gave her a hug and a quick kiss that made them both feel a special connection. They said goodnight and David headed toward his parents' car. Becky decided to join a couple of her friends for the walk to her house. David watched her as long as he could from the rear window of his parents' Buick. On the way home, he struggled with not being more honest with Becky. In his heart he wanted to tell her everything that he had experienced today. He hoped that somehow he would figure out what was going on and then he could explain it to Becky and everyone so that it made sense. He hoped.

David bounced out of bed this morning to do his chores, even though it was now part of the Christmas holiday break and there was no school to worry about for a couple of weeks. It was December 22 and the family was making the annual trek into the big city of Spokane, Washington, across the Idaho-Washington border, for their annual Christmas shopping spree. David was so excited thinking about the idea of his parents actually getting him a car that he felt a little guilty. But he also enjoyed buying things for his parents and siblings. He had saved his money from chores and odd jobs at neighboring farms, so he was anxious to go to the big department stores in downtown Spokane and shop for some nice gifts.

He hurried through the milking session this morning and even annoyed some of the cows as he rushed them through the process. Because there was no school, he finished the entire herd, with his dad helping him with the final group of cows. They got all the equipment and the milking parlor cleaned once the last cow was finished. The cows settled into their routine of eating and spending the day relaxing and huddling together to keep warm. They would probably be milked a bit later than usual tonight because of the family shopping excursion, but they were oblivious to that at this point. There had been a light snow overnight, and it was still snowing this morning but only lightly. However, a thick blanket of fog had settled over the valley and visibility was less than fifty feet.

David was in a good mood and was whistling as he finished the last of his chores and exited the milking parlor on his way to the house and some well-earned breakfast. Thoughts of the strange man had faded a bit from his mind. As he started toward the house through the fog, his heart was light with anticipation of the joys of the day ahead. What was Christmas anyway but the anticipation of gifts and time together? As he made his way along the fog-shrouded path, he noticed footprints in the snow headed away from the house and into the fog. The footprints were fresh and were clearly not his dad's. He stopped to study them. It was curious because fresh snowflakes were just making their mark in the footprints, so he knew they were made only in the last few minutes. He slowly raised his gaze in the direction of the footprints and as he did, he caught sight of someone, or something, just disappearing into the fog. He thought about going to find his dad but his curiosity propelled him forward. As he walked slowly ahead, he could not help but think about the man he had seen before and that this must be connected.

As he pondered this, he looked again at the footprints. They were the size of a man's footprint but strange because they were flat and featureless, not the kind of print that would be left by a winter boot with a cleated sole. They did not even look like the print from a regular shoe. As he studied the footprints, he started to become anxious. Was he losing his mind? He did not really want to see this man again, but the need to know more was overpowering, so he continued his pursuit into the fog, following closely the odd but ominous footprints in the fresh snow.

He was not really aware of how long he had been tracking the footprints as he continued his search for the owner. Behind him the fog quickly enshrouded the barn and house and he found himself enveloped in it, with only the footprints to accompany him. He proceeded cautiously and was now feeling a bit foolish. Why didn't he bring his dad with him, instead of tracking this himself?

It was snowing harder now and becoming more difficult to see ahead on the trail of footprints. He kept shifting his gaze from the footprints to the barely visible trail in front of him. He had learned from his hunting experience to make sure he swept his gaze across the horizon in case his prey was circling around or shifting directions in front of him. He had learned this the hard way while tracking a large buck deer in a light snowstorm. The buck had circled around and while David was looking ahead, the Buck got a good look at David from the side and with that, he was gone. David realized it just as the buck bolted away from him. He had not made that mistake again and was not going to make it today.

Suddenly there was color within the swirls of snow. Yes, it was a person just ahead in the fog and snowstorm. David stopped in his tracks to try to see the body better, but whoever it was made a quick exit into the white shroud of swirling snow. David could picture the figure of the mystery man and a quick shiver traveled down his back. He stopped for just a second or two to try to rationalize this crazy adventure he found himself in. He realized that there was not time for reflection if he wanted to get to the bottom of this strange string of events. Taking a deep breath of cold winter air and a full measure of resolve, and with some good old-fashioned farmer's grit, he hurried ahead to try to catch the man.

He scrambled ahead about 200 feet when through the fog and snow he found himself staring at the strange man. David stopped short. The man was about fifty feet in front of him and partially hidden in snow and fog but clearly visible enough to see that it was the same man. He was facing David and staring directly at him. He wore the same tunic and held a staff, a walking stick, really. The man was not tall, probably average height, and of medium build. He looked strong in the shoulders and chest, even though he was somewhat slight. The man's tunic was a pattern of weaved cloth with white sleeves and a rainbow of colors along the body of the tunic. What appeared to be a blanket before was more of an outer garment or wrap. Whatever dress this man had on was clearly not designed for winters in the panhandle of Northern Idaho. It looked much too lightweight. The man's facial expression was that same smile that forgot to tell the mouth to join in. The man once again was shaking his head side to side as if disapproving David.

David had an overwhelming urge to run toward him and tackle him. But he could not run. He could not even force his feet to even think about moving. They were in the same state of transfixion as the rest of his body. It seemed that only his eyes and mind were functioning.

Even though David's extremities were immobile, his mouth was functional. "Who are you? What do you want? Why do you keep bothering me?" David found himself shouting spontaneously into the harsh December wind. His voice sounded contrite but feeble out here in the snowstorm. In answer, the man only shook his head more emphatically as David shouted.

The man slowly looked skyward and spread his arms as one might do in the sunshine on the first warm day of spring. This struck David as particularly peculiar, as this was obviously not a warm spring day. David stopped shouting, as it was obvious that the man was not going to respond. The man slowly raised his hands over his head until they were clasped together in a prayer-like position and pointing straight up to the sky. David could only watch and ponder this strange encounter.

Very slowly the man lowered his arms, all the while holding his penetrating gaze straight on David. His expression slowly changed to one of a stern face, like a father who is upset with his child's behavior.

The man and David held each other's gaze for an undeterminable amount of time as the snow and fog swirled between them. In time, the man dropped his gaze, turned into the storm, and disappeared in a blanket of fog and snow. David was left standing alone, filled with disquiet. Although his feet felt like lead weights, he forced them to come to life and started to pursue the menacing apparition. David did not know where his resolve was coming from as he picked up speed and quickly reached the spot where the stranger had stood. He looked at the ground to see where the tracks were leading, just like he had learned to do on so many hunting trips with his dad.

Somehow he was not surprised to see that the tracks stopped just before where the man had stood, and where he had been standing there were no tracks at all. Not a mark in the snow to indicate anyone had been standing there just mere seconds before. He resisted what his eyes were seeing and raised his head to study the swirling fog ahead in a vain search for his tormentor. As he stared into the bleak winter morning, he wasn't sure whether he was angry or frightened, or maybe both, and he started to shiver in the storm. He could not pull himself away from this physical point. While his mind raced, his body just continued to shiver and shake with anxiety. He knew there must be some logical explanation for his experiences with this apparition. Yes, he thought, an apparition is what this was for him. It was clear now that this was not a normal person, not with all these strange appearances and, more disturbingly, disappearances. With his Catholic Church upbringing, he started to wonder if this was some kind of punishment for something he had done or maybe not done in his past. He continued to ponder this seemingly impossible set of circumstances and, more importantly, the undeniable evidence of what he had witnessed. Being a student of science, he mentally worked his mind through the potential possibilities of how this was happening. He knew that this was not a normal person and it seemed clear that he was the only one seeing this person. He continued to race through the possibilities but had to force his mind to slow down to better analyze and consider the most likely scenarios. He considered that this was maybe just a vision, an apparition that was somehow appearing only to him. That just seemed too farfetched for him to seriously consider, so he dismissed that possibility, or attempted to. He thought about the past and whether he had suffered a head injury at some point that might account for such visions. Although like most children, he had his encounters with bumps and bruises, he could not really identify a serious enough head injury to account for what he was experiencing. It seemed the more he tried to figure it out, the more confusing it became.

"David!" A faint voice cut through the fog and swirl of snow. It took David just a minute to break his trance and realize his dad was calling him. He suddenly felt embarrassed because he didn't know how he would explain such ridiculous events to his always practical and pragmatic father. He knew instantly that he would not be able to explain it, so he decided he would not even mention it. He immediately started to consider what he would tell his dad. He turned toward where he heard the voice, but he did not immediately respond. He needed more time to contemplate his situation.

"David, where are you?" his father called again. David shouted back that he was fine and was just walking back toward the house. At least he hoped he was walking toward the house. The ground was flat and opaque in the storm, so although he knew the farm as well as anyone, he was away from his familiar trails and normal landmarks and was not entirely certain of his orientation. He shouted again to his dad, hoping to elicit enough of a response to provide some audio radar guidance back to the comfort and safety of the house. Heck, even the milk house would be a welcome sight at this point. His dad responded in more of a scold than an offer of assistance, the kind of scolding voice that parents often use when children engage in something dangerously foolish but survive unharmed. David aligned his gait to his father's voice and made his way back quickly to the warmth and familiar comfort of the house.

"What in heck were you doing out in that awful snowstorm, David?" His father quizzed him as they met face-to-face on the back stoop of the house.

"I thought that I saw something in the storm, you know, an animal or something. I thought that it might be hurt or lost, so I went to check it out." David's rapid ability to forge together this quick lie surprised even him. He was not accustomed to lying to his parents, and so this felt foreign and uncomfortable. He did not like lying to his dad this way. His dad had always been his idol. He gave David a sideways stare with one eyebrow raised, clearly studying him to analyze this unusual story from his normally very reliable son. David was able to manufacture enough of an innocent, honest face to defer any further questions, although not suspicions, from his father.

43

Back inside the house, the family chatted excitedly over a large breakfast as they anticipated the day's journey into Spokane for the annual Christmas shopping trek. Although David participated in the conversation, he didn't feel the same enthusiasm as the rest of the family because the latest encounter with the man had shaken him. He shivered a bit when he thought about this latest vanishing episode. He tried to collect his thoughts around the coming day's adventure and had some limited success making small talk with his youngest sister. Her animation about shopping and Christmas in the city was enough to help him bridge back to reality from his private thoughts.

The drive to Spokane in the family's Buick station wagon turned out to be an adventure in itself. The storm had turned the roads quite slippery and all the cars were driving well below the speed limit in order to keep control. Paul Edmonds was a very experienced driver and even in these conditions was very skilled at keeping the vehicle under control and his family safe. He knew the keys to controlling the vehicle were maintaining a safe speed, paying close attention to other vehicles, and staying off the brakes in any kind of an icy skid. Although Janet Edmonds was always nervous driving in snowstorms, she trusted her husband's ability at the wheel in this kind of weather. The children were oblivious to the inherent dangers on a public highway during such weather. Their minds were absorbed with the coming activities. David found himself feeling detached and mostly looking out the window at the storm and passing cars. He had never experienced anything like this before and was at a loss as to how to respond to it, or more accurately, how to understand it. The flying snow helped to hypnotize him enough to take his mind off his situation. When they finally started to drive out of the storm and the clouds broke enough for intermittent sun splashes on the new white wonderland, he found he was starting to forget the events of the morning and now was looking forward to getting to the city and doing some shopping.

As Spokane is southwest of Seltice Falls, the storm had passed through it earlier in the day and left a white and magical blanket of Christmas snow. The anticipation in the car was electric, as the sight of the new fallen snow on the seasonally anointed city created a wonderland scene. Paul Edmonds wound the station wagon through the city streets and the traffic that, by big city standards was modest, but compared to Seltice Falls was something to observe in awe. Mr. Edmonds navigated to the main parking area in the downtown section of the city and exhaled a sigh of relief when he shut down the engine after many miles on a snowy, slippery highway, followed by heavy city traffic. "All right, gang, we are here. Let's plan our shopping exploits so that we don't get lost in the crowds," he stated emphatically toward the windshield.

They hurriedly formed a plan of attack on how to work the shops without exposing the secret treasures to the planned recipients. David and his mom planned to go to the Crescent Department Store to find some gifts for his dad and his sister, Katy. Mr. Edmonds and the younger ones would head out on their own secret mission to find the right gifts for Mrs. Edmonds and David. Mr. Edmonds had the difficult task of coaching the younger ones on being sure not to say too much about what was being purchased, which was sometimes an impossible task.

They agreed to meet at the Apple Tree restaurant in the Crescent Department Store for lunch, and from there they would decide on the next mission assignment. David and his mother did the obligatory shopping at the Crescent, buying some nice clothes for his dad, as well as a new Seiko watch for him for church and other formal outings.

David's mom wanted some time at the store to shop without David looking over her shoulder, so she asked him to go explore on his own before lunch. David could not have been happier, as department store shopping was not a real priority for him.

David headed out of the Crescent onto Riverside Avenue and turned west toward the Sears & Roebuck at the end of the block. He wanted to check out the outdoor gear there, as well as what they might have for sports equipment. Although he was not a sports nut, he loved examining the equipment. As he made his way along Riverside Avenue in the brisk winter chill, he remembered how much he loved being in the city and observing all the activity. There was so much more here to see and do than in Seltice Falls. He walked with his head swinging from side to side, trying to take in all the sights and sounds of the street, the bustling people on their Christmas adventures, and the glow of the department store windows onto the sidewalk in the low-hanging light of the short winter day. He had almost forgotten the morning's sighting of the man and felt again like a young teenager on an adventure. His pace felt brisker and more energetic than earlier in the day, and the gloomy shroud that enveloped him on the drive to Spokane had lifted. As he traversed in front of the Crescent's imposing storefront, he quickly came upon a small gathering of gaiety in front of a large, plate-glass window in the storefront. As he piloted around the crowd of happy humans, he paused to see what was capturing their attention and uplifting their spirits. He peered over the adult heads directly in front of him and saw that most of the happy audience was children. He got a clear view of what was entertaining the crowd; it was the annual Christmas display in the Crescent window. Elves were riding in overhead mining-type cars carrying all sorts of scaled-down toys and packages. The background sky was twinkling with stars and, quite illogically, it was snowing from this cloudless sky. Of course, there was a barber pole marked as the North Pole, just in case someone could not conclude the location from the display. There was a large, red gingerbread house in the middle of the display that had several backlit windows, as well as a sign over the wooden, Dutch-style door that said, "Workshop." As if to keep the magic alive, there was no direct sighting of Santa, but in the shadows of the largest of the Workshop's windows, there was a clear silhouette of the jolly elf reading from an old-style scroll, no doubt the naughty-and-nice list.

David was beyond the Santa years, of course, but the enchantment of the scene held his attention, and he found himself smiling and laughing with the rest of the group. As he was enjoying the scene, his eye caught sight of something to his immediate right. His gut immediately contracted and the smile left his face. He pivoted his head in a hard right turn, and before he could fully absorb what had grabbed him, the comfort of the crowd and the merry scene quickly evaporated into the cold air. He felt himself go cold as he caught sight of the man ahead of him walking down Riverside Avenue, heading toward the Sears store. The man was moving through the crowd unnoticed, except to David, of course. David instinctively broke from the display window crowd and started in the direction of the man. He quickened his pace and began to close the gap between himself and the man. He could see the long hair that was an anomaly on this street of seasonal shoppers. He found that his quickened pace, although effective to close the gap, was annoying to others on the street as he pushed past them, bumping shoulders with those moving with the flow.

As the distance closed between the man and David, David slowed his approach. He was not sure what he was going to do when he caught up to him. More importantly, he was unsure what this man would do. Would he vanish again right here in the middle of this bustling crowd? Was David the only one that could see this guy?

Following close behind the man, he matched his pace step for step as they walked briskly down the street toward the Sears store. David had lost his focus on Sears and focused his icy gaze on the back of the man's head, where his shaggy hair bounced with each step. David analyzed the man and noticed that this time he was wearing a long winter coat instead of the tunic and blanket he wore on the previous occasions. The man also seemed taller than before, but David could not really be sure, as the past encounters were so brief. David thought about ignoring him and continuing on to Sears to continue his shopping, but he knew immediately that he could not break away from this pursuit.

David took a deep breath and quickened his pace to close the gap with the man and confront him. He knew this was what he had to do. He could not continue to let this person haunt him uncontested. As he reached the man, he raised his arm slowly and reached out to the man's right shoulder. He noticed his hand was trembling and he could feel sweat beads forming on his forehead. His arm was out in front of him and he could clearly see it was his arm but in his field of view, the arm in front of him looked like it must belong to someone else. His mind was struggling to confront what his optic nerves were telling him. His hand hovered for a moment over the man's shoulder as he contemplated gripping the shoulder and turning the man around.

He did not get the opportunity to even touch the man as his hovering hand was seen peripherally by the man, and to David's horror, the man quickly stopped and turned to confront him.

He looked straight into David's face and barked, "What do you want?" Both David and the man stopped suddenly in the middle of the sidewalk as holiday shoppers navigated around them with annoyed expressions. "What?" the man repeated as they locked stares.

David gasped as he realized this was not the man at all! He had mistaken him for the strange man, but except for the long hair and beard, this guy did not look anything like the man he had seen before. David stepped back as he absorbed his sudden embarrassment. People walking by were now slowing to see what was going on between these two people. David could not speak as he stared at the man. He could not help but wonder if the man could change his looks as part of his experience. Was this the same guy or was David just completely mistaken here?

"Kid, you better go back to your mommy," the man said flatly and turned to continue toward Sears. David just stood and watched him walk away. He was in a mild state of shock, both from originally thinking this was another encounter with the man and from the realization that he was completely mistaken and had almost gotten himself into serious trouble. He stood for a long time on the sidewalk as the holiday crowds wound around him. He did not even take notice of them; he could only watch as the longhaired man shrank into the distance. The man did not look back but kept going until he disappeared into one of the many storefronts on Riverside Avenue. David thought about how he had put himself into this awkward situation and could not help but think that he needed to be more careful.

He slowly made his way toward Sears, although he did not remember why he was walking in that direction. He watched people hurry past him on their way toward the different shops. He had completely forgotten his plan or purpose. He was lost in his thoughts, fear, anxiety, and bewilderment. He felt all alone in this maddening experience. He wanted to share this with someone, almost anyone, but he did not know how to frame the conversation without sounding mad. His mom had always been the cornerstone he could lean on when he needed to share personal struggles and challenges. She could listen with the ear of a counselor and the wisdom of a sage. Her advice was always kind and respectful, and even when criticism was part of the discussion, it was always delivered with care. He loved his dad but speaking with him always seemed like work and the outcome seemed to be unfinished. His dad was always too quick to provide tired clichés related to life's challenges.

He continued walking without a destination. His eyes were taking in the sights and his ears the sounds, but his mind wasn't interested in the incoming information. His mind was busy shuffling through the myriad thoughts and emotions from the last few days. He wanted to find a phone and call Becky, and tell her everything that had happened to him. He felt sure Becky would listen and comfort him, and somehow explain it all to him so that it would make sense. He began to imagine the conversation in his mind. He could feel a veil of comfort descend over him as he tried to hear Becky's voice in his mind.

He found himself walking into the Sears store and his trance faded into the warmth of the store's festive foyer. He walked slowly through the store and mostly forgot about the tool section and outdoor goods. He wandered back outside and toward his prearranged rendezvous with his mom. As he strolled down the street, he saw a beautiful 1955 Chevrolet Bel Air moving slowly down the street, and his mind raced back to his dream of getting a car from his parents for Christmas. This interlude helped bring him back to the present moment and relieved him of some of his painful reflection.

The day's shopping ended in the typical fashion, with lots of gifts being purchased, followed by lunch at a restaurant and some time spent exploring the city. Janet Edmonds's mothering instincts took in the somber mood of David during the rest of the day. Although she did not question David about his demeanor, she kept a watchful eye on him. She had not forgotten the still-unexplained episode at the basketball game the night before. Janet kept her thoughts and fears to herself for the rest of the outing and on the long drive home. As the snowstorm had passed, the travel back to Seltice Falls was uneventful and somewhat boring after the busy day.

Although the family got home a bit late, David called Becky as soon as he arrived. He had to be discreet, as there was only one phone in the house and it was near the kitchen, where conversations tended to be public. David knew his mom's hearing was somehow superior when listening to his conversations involving the phone and young ladies.

David was relieved when it was Becky who answered. They exchanged pleasantries and chatted about the day's activities. In David's case that meant only the activities that did not include encounters with strange, bearded men. Becky had spent the morning helping her mom catch up on household chores that included laundry and the like. Then they had spent the snowy afternoon in a cozy kitchen baking Christmas cookies, some homemade chocolate candy, and a few other sweets that would not only adorn their home and palates this season, but also would be gifts to some lucky friends and neighbors. Somewhere during this chatty small talk, David blurted out that he wanted to know if Becky could get away tonight and see him for few minutes.

Becky was caught by surprise but she recovered quickly, saying, "David, you know I would like to see you, but it is a bit late and I have not talked to Mom at all about going out tonight." She quickly added, "But let me ask her and see what she says. What should I tell her about this? Anything?"

David had already been less than honest with his dad and he surely did not want to get into a bad relationship with Becky's mom. In fact, he liked Becky's mom a great deal and was immediately troubled by feeling that he had to quickly work on another falsehood. "Just tell her that I had a long day and wanted to visit for a few minutes. Really, I will have you home in no time, promise."

"Sure, easy for you to say. You don't have to be the one convincing her!" Becky retorted. "OK, let me talk to her, and I'll call you back either way."

"Thanks, Becky. It's important to me," David said in such a serious voice that it made Becky feel uneasy, as if she was being drawn into something more sinister than a simple visit with a lonely teenage boy on a Saturday night, and of course she was.

Becky's mom was suspicious but she liked David and knew his parents well, which included admiration for them and their demonstrated strong characters, as well as friendly personalities. Since the loss of her husband, Mary Marston was understandably a bit overcautious in regard to her children and their safety. She knew the knife-like pain of losing someone that was so much a part of her life and her being. Slithering beneath the surface of her psyche was the real fear that another such loss might push her to lose her grip on sanity. She did not want to find out the blackness of such a reality. However, she was also a pragmatist and knew that her children had to grow to adults and, as such, had to experience life, albeit with risks and pains included. Exhaling a long sigh and with a keen sense of unease, she gave her tacit approval for Becky to see David regardless. This was part of Mary's inner strength, given that she would probably be more comfortable keeping her children locked in the house where she could ensure their safety.

Becky sensed the torment in her mother's demeanor and gave her a light kiss on the cheek and touched her shoulder. With that, she gave a broad smile as she whisked away to the front window to watch for the familiar headlights of the Edmonds's family station wagon. She did not have to wait long before the night was pierced with the rays of light glowing off the snow and swinging into the Marston driveway. David was there. Becky's heart raced just a bit and she felt a slight flutter in her stomach in anticipation of seeing him. He had sounded so serious about getting together, and she wanted to be able to soothe him. She wanted to hug his anxiety away, even though she did not really know how serious it was.

David met her at the door as Becky gave a quick smile and said good-bye to her mom, who also put on a smile that was clearly manufactured for the occasion. They kissed lightly and both got into the car from the driver's door. Becky sat close to David as he slowly backed the car into the street and made sure he drove away slowly so as not to upset Mrs. Marston. They drove to a vacant parking lot at the local doctor's office, where it was quiet and they could be alone. He left the motor running as the night air was very cold and he did not want Becky to be uncomfortable. As for himself, he felt flushed and overheated trying to fabricate the best way to talk to Becky about his dilemma.

They made some small talk in the warmth of the car. David chatted about Spokane and shopping, and Becky talked about being stuck in boring old Seltice Falls all day with some Christmas baking to keep her company. David mentioned the beautiful Chevy Bel Air he had seen in Spokane. He chatted about how nice it would be for them to be in his car instead of his parents' car. Becky nodded, but she was just happy to be with David, no matter the car. Thus far, the real topic of this unusual rendezvous stayed out of the conversation, but it was not lost on Becky that there was an elephant in the room, for both of them. David felt the conversation starting to wane and he knew he had to reach out to her. He did not want to face the strange man alone any longer.

"Becky, I need to speak to you about something that is kind of weird, but I can only tell you if you absolutely promise not to tell anyone. I mean anyone, or I could be in serious trouble." David blurted this out into the quiet space between them and Becky started to laugh, thinking he was being a bit overdramatic. She quickly caught herself when she met his eyes and could see something deadly serious in David's stare. Becky wasn't sure but she thought she could see fear in his eyes, which was not something she was used to finding there. "I really need to be able to trust you on this, Becky. I can't have anyone else knowing about it," David continued, and as he finished, he locked a penetrating stare straight into Becky's eyes. "Do you understand?"

Becky held his gaze. "David, what is going on? Are you in some kind of trouble that you should be speaking to your parents about?"

David looked toward the windshield in a blank stare. "No, I'm not in trouble, well, at least I don't think so, and it's not really something I'm comfortable telling my parents about. They would get all weird about it and my dad would think I was nuts or something. I don't really know how to explain it except to just tell you about it." He paused and looked at Becky again as he continued. "I can't tell you unless I know my secret is safe with you, at least until I can figure out what is going on with me. What do you think?"

Becky exhaled and sat silent for a moment as she thought about her ability to keep such a secret when she did not even know what it was about. What if keeping the secret could bring harm to David or his family or someone else. Of course, she wanted to know what this was about, but she was also a person of character, like her mother, and would not make such a promise lightly. Becky was smart and considered her options on how to meet David's request while still keeping a safety net in place in case this situation became dangerous. She decided to negotiate a bit before making the commitment. "David, you have to tell me that by making this promise of secrecy to you that I am not endangering anyone, including you. I can't keep quiet if it means that some harm could come to you or anyone else."

"Becky, I don't think there is anything like that involved here. Of course, I can't be sure because I don't know myself what is really going on. I guess you will just have to trust me," David responded.

"OK, then we have to agree that if we determine there is a real danger in this, we will notify our parents." Becky felt this seemed reasonable.

"Well, we both have to agree that there is danger and we need to get help. We have to decide together and not just one of us on our own, OK?" David countered.

"Somehow I feel that I'm not getting the best deal here, but OK, I agree," Becky said with a grimace. "What is your secret problem, then?"

David took a deep breath and started talking. He told Becky about the strange man and what happened in the milk parlor before school and at the basketball game. He told her about the man in the snowstorm and how he vanished when David caught up to him. She listened quietly and only interrupted him a couple of times with questions. When he was finished, he said, "I really need to work this out myself, at least for now, and I know it will help me if I can confide in you about it."

"Well, of course, I'm flattered that you feel comfortable confiding in me about it. That said, I'm not really that comfortable with this information. Frankly, it frightens me. I mean, you are seeing this strange man and no one else can see him? Good heavens, David, that is Hollywood fiction stuff, for crying out loud," Becky responded.

"Yeah, I know, but can you imagine if this story got out and around this small town? I might as well pack my bags, because everyone in town would have me in the loony bin for sure. I need to figure this out for myself first. I'm just not ready to let this out, and you can understand that, right?" David pleaded.

"Of course, I can understand your concerns, but that assumes that this is really something that is happening and not some medical condition that could be really serious. I'm not sure this is fair to me to have this burden to carry when I don't know how I can help," Becky said to the darkness in the night. She continued. "I will keep my promise, of course, but only if it is obvious that your health or safety is not in danger, OK?"

"Now don't forget our agreement includes mutual consent to disclose this to anyone else, right?" David's voice had some concern in it for Becky's loyalty.

"I will honor my promise," Becky paused. "Well, up to a point. I'm not going to let something bad happen to you, David. I love you, you stupid jerk!" Becky shot back, not really meaning to let the "L" word slip out, as this had so far been an unspoken term between them. She actually felt relief at putting her feelings on the line. The current situation seemed to demand that their relationship take a step toward maturity.

David sat quiet for a moment as they both stared straight ahead into the night and the empty parking lot. It was not tension in the air but rather almost clearing of the air regarding their feelings toward each other. Both being responsible young people, they had taken their parents' advice that they were probably too young to be in love, but somehow they now transcended that advice and formed an instant bond of honesty that required transparency. With no words, they found themselves in a velvety kiss and embrace that made it clear David's secret was safe now. Their embrace felt completely new, even though they had hugged each other before. The bond they formed now with their bodies held closely together had a purpose beyond their own selfish teenage stirrings. The warmth between them was not just of body temperature, but of trust and dedication that neither had known with anyone, outside of their parents. Neither of them wanted to separate from this physical and emotional bond. They shared another kiss and continued to hold each other as they returned to their conversation.

They discussed the visions some more, and David added as much detail as he could remember, which lifted a weight from his emotional baggage that had become uncomfortably heavy the past few days. David even told Becky about his embarrassment regarding approaching the man in Spokane who was not the man at all. Becky laughed at the thought of David's red face when he realized he was accosting a stranger on a street of Christmas shoppers.

"Oh, David, I have to get home. Look at the time," Becky said suddenly as she looked at David's watch. "My mom is not going to be happy with me being out this late."

"Do you want me to come into the house and apologize to her?" David offered. He quickly continued, "Remember that what I told you is absolutely a strict secret."

Becky declined this offer as she felt she knew much better than David how to best manage her mom. She gave her allegiance to their pact of secrecy, although she was slightly bothered by his crisis of faith in her earlier commitment to their shared secret.

David drove Becky home, and they parted with an unusually heartfelt kiss and a promise that David would let Becky know about any additional strange appearances. They both knew that their relationship had just taken a step beyond teenage infatuation.

Becky entered her house quickly to escape the cold night, but once inside she watched as David navigated out of the narrow driveway and the lights of the Buick receded into the night. She stood and stared at the darkness that quickly enveloped the street and pondered the conversation with David. She was not sure what to make of his story or situation, but his confiding in her gave her new and sweeter feelings for him and the word love came to mind, a word that she had tried to keep at bay as she wanted to keep her focus on school and her future. This episode seemed to change their relationship into something more. She did not even know the words to describe it, but indeed, her heart did not need mere words for her to embrace her enhanced feelings toward David.

She made sure she said goodnight to her mom and gave her a kiss on the cheek. Her mom, of course, was wide-awake listening for the safe return of her daughter.

"Did you have a nice time, honey?" Mary Marston semi-whispered into the darkened bedroom. "It seemed like a strange time for going out."

"David is just having some difficult times right now with some things and just wanted to speak about it with someone, that's all." Becky could never lie to her mom so she did her best to provide a selective truth without exposing David's real problems.

"OK, dear, I hope everything is all right. I'm glad you're home now and I love you. Please get straight to bed as it's getting late," her mom said and, to Becky's relief, did not engage in any further questioning.

Becky snuggled under the large quilt and cold sheets in her room and could not help but stare at the ceiling in quiet contemplation of the conversation with David. It was completely out of character for David to make up such a yarn, or have such an experience, assuming this was true. Still, Becky could not bring herself to believe that David had been anything but completely honest about his experiences. She knew full well, too, how difficult it must have been for him to open up to her about it. Although her heart was aflutter with being in his confidence, it was also troubled by the burden of this knowledge and the pledge of confidence with David. What if it continued and she really needed to let his parents know? Her thoughts kept sleep away for almost an hour, but finally the fatigue of the day made its way into Becky's conscious and she drifted into a deep sleep.

David loved to drive, even the family's ugly station wagon. He usually enjoyed going fast, but tonight was different. He eased the big Buick wagon out of Becky's driveway, under the watchful eye of Mary Marston from her bedroom, and found himself slowly motoring down the street toward home. He kept a slow pace as he pondered the wisdom of baring his soul to Becky. He didn't feel regret, but he did reconsider the wisdom of his decision. He could not help wondering again if maybe he was really losing his mind, or worse, maybe Becky thought he was going crazy. Would her concern overwhelm her promise and compel her to speak to her mom, or to her friends? His mind raced back and forth about his situation. In a strange way, he almost hoped that Becky might out him to his parents and force the issue, saving him from making such a decision. His uncertainty about all of this was more than he could think about all at once. He tried to focus once again on that 1955 Chevy he hoped to get for Christmas.

Just as he made the turn out of town onto the rural road toward the Edmonds dairy farm, the headlights of the Buick flashed upon the familiar figure in the middle of the road. The headlights squared up on the figure, and time seemed to stop. The bright lights gave the scene the feel of a photograph rather than real life. The man was unmistakable, the long hair, unkempt and slightly ragged beard, rainbow tunic, and sardonic facial expression.

The suddenness of the man's appearance caused David to instinctively hit the brake pedal, and the drum brakes on the big Buick quickly locked up the wheels on the ice-coated country road. The Buick went into an immediate slide with the driver's side careening toward the left side road ditch. David's limited experience on such an icy road caused him to only press the brakes harder, which aggravated the skid. He did not yet have the instincts to steer into the skid and allow the car to right itself. His dad would have just as instinctively turned into the skid and only tapped the brakes, but Paul Edmonds had many years of winter driving experience and, of course, he did not have the challenge of dealing with apparitions.

The ditch was filled with a snow berm from the plows that filled the depression that would normally be on the side of the road in any season except winter. The helpless Buick was doing all its pilot was commanding but could only continue toward the frozen snowbank with all four wheels locked tight. Although David's speed was modest, the weight of the big Buick plowed into the waiting and impartial berm of snow with both a thud and a crunch that sounded sickening to David and quickly came to a stop. The headlights were now only illuminating the berm as the Buick stopped at a thirty-degree angle to the flow of traffic. David was not normally inclined to profanity but he shouted, "Shit!" so loudly that he startled himself.

The driver's door was wedged against the snow berm. David fumbled through the glove box to find the flashlight that his dad always kept at the ready in the car. He made his way out the passenger door, flashlight in hand, and quickly pointed it in the direction of where the man had been standing. But no one was there, just an empty, icy road. He scanned down the road and the berms on both sides, straining his eyes against the darkness to find his nemesis. He wanted to shout and scream at this guy! How could this be happening to him? He looked for tracks in the snow on the side of the road to see if the man had escaped into the fields, but of course there was nothing, and the road itself was too frozen to leave footprints.

Dejectedly he eyed his vehicle and its out-of-place position in the road. He slowly walked around the front of the car to view the driver's front fender that had impacted the snowbank. He was frightened to look and already envisioned what kinds of dents and scratches awaited him that would require some kind of plausible explanation to his dad. He could not help but consider that this might sink his hopes of getting a car this Christmas. How could he expect his dad to come through when he was running their station wagon into a snowbank? He put the flashlight to work inspecting the left front fender. To his absolute delight, he could not see any visible damage. But his delight was quickly overshadowed by his predicament of being stuck in a snowbank on a deserted road in late December in Northern Idaho. He spent considerable time inspecting the errant fender and found some mars and slight scratches, but he felt confident that these were already there, or at least he could probably convince his dad of this scenario.

Once he was satisfied that the Buick was no worse for wear, he started to study his situation with more vigor. Fortunately for David, their neighbor and fellow dairy farmer, Del Newberry, came rolling down the road and to a slow stop opposite the marooned Buick. David liked Mr. Newberry enough, but he knew him to always deliver his sarcastic wit whenever such so-called wit could reach its most irritating zenith.

Following a methodical and purposeful slow roll down of the driver's window, Mr. Newberry eyed the stranded Buick and David in one roving and humorless glance. Almost on cue, Del Newberry droned, "Looks like we got ourselves a new driver here." After a calculated pause, he continued. "Boy, your daddy would not like to see his nice Buick in the ditch like that, ya know." After this dreadfully obvious comment, he zeroed his eyes on David. "What's your plan here, Mr. David?" he continued.

Although David wanted to respond with an equally obvious and sarcastic remark, he knew Mr. Newberry to be his elder and could only remark, "I suspect I will have to depend on the good graces of someone like you, Mr. Newberry, to assist me in getting this out of the ditch."

"You think so! Well, if I didn't respect your parents so much, I might let you figure this out for yourself, but I suppose I will have to help you out." Mr. Newberry grunted.

With that, the two of them were able to push, rock, and spin the Buick free of the snowbank. David was soon on his way home. Once the focus of getting the Buick free was out of his mind, he again contemplated that he had seen the specter again, but this time because it had been for only a brief second, he started to doubt what he had seen in those headlights. He thought about calling Becky again, but he wasn't sure if she believed him at all, which left him with the dilemma of trying to decide if she was really his confidant in this strange string of events that he found himself enveloped. This left him feeling alone again without a way to take any action.

After confessing cleanly to his dad about the slide into the ditch, minus the specter, he settled into bed and spent a fitful night tossing and turning. Tomorrow would be another day, whether good or bad, he could not even guess.

Chapter 6

The morning dawned clear and cold. The storm had passed and left the sky free to hang some stars. David rose early as he always did to do his milking chores, even before Sunday morning mass. Although he had a restless night, he welcomed the dawn of the new day and the sunshine that would soon disperse the night. He dressed in his milking clothes and made his way through the kitchen and out into the cold, crisp December air. As he passed through the kitchen, he could smell the aroma of the fresh pot of coffee his mom had made.

Yesterday's snow was now frozen and made a crunching sound as his footsteps marched toward the milk house. With the short December days in Northern Idaho, the sun was still waiting to rise for the day and darkness still had the upper hand. The fringes of daylight, however, combined with the blanket of new white snow allowed David to scan the horizon in all directions for his nemesis. Not seeing anything out of the ordinary, he made his way to the familiar surroundings of the milking parlor. The normal sights and sounds of the stanchions, the cows moving into queue, and the milking machinery were like familiar old friends this morning and gave him some peace. He even started to hum a favorite Christmas carol as he set about the milking operation. It went smoothly enough and without any interruption from the apparition or any other unwelcome intrusions. The normalcy of the morning's operation was a great relief to him. The cows even sensed his calm demeanor and seemed to relax and even enjoy the process of being relieved of their overfull udders.

As he approached the final group of cows in the queue, his dad joined him in the parlor and helped him finish. They worked together to clean the milking machinery, the milk bearing piping, the stanchions where the cows traversed, and the large bulk tank that stored the morning's milk.

On Sundays, the family readied for mass right after chores were completed, rather than take their breakfast. This always troubled David, as his teenage appetite did not easily adapt to this deviation from the normal schedule. He knew that this belated breakfast was not negotiable, however, so he dutifully went about taking a quick shower and changing into his Sunday mass clothes, along with the rest of the family. Once everyone was ready, they piled into the Buick and made their way into town toward the local Catholic Church. The early mass was at 8:00 and usually drew a larger congregation in this farming community than the 10:00 mass, which was for those who wished to sleep in a bit later or did not finish their farm chores as early as the Edmonds family. David had to do his regular turn at being an altar server, which rotated among the teenage boys of the parish. Although he did not mind doing the chore of altar server, he was glad that he did not have to take on the task on this Sunday morning. He wasn't sure why but with the strange encounters of the past few days, he felt more comfortable just spending the time at mass quietly with his family.

David's desires for such a quiet mass with his family were quickly disrupted. As he approached the steps of the church, he saw Ronnie Hovett approaching him. David had known Ronnie for many years, and although they were not really friends, they got along with each other well enough. Ronnie was a year older than David and so he held some seniority, or perceived seniority, regarding the altar servers' pecking order.

"David, Johnny Bates is sick today and I need you to substitute for him as the other server. I don't have anyone else who knows what to do and can step in for Johnny," Ronnie blurted straight into David's face.

David stepped back from Ronnie to give some space between them and fix his gaze into Ronnie's eyes. David's gaze indicated clearly that he did not want to be drafted into altar serving this morning. Ronnie stepped forward again and repeated his plea for David's assistance at the altar.

"Ronnie, you know this is not my week to serve. Isn't there someone else that can step in this morning?" David pleaded. Ronnie was not to be denied this day and made his case for David's assistance. David could see that his resistance was futile, so he reluctantly acquiesced to Ronnie's pleas and let his mother know that he would be serving at mass today and would not be able to sit with the family. His mother was supportive and gave him encouragement to assist with the service as requested.

David quickly made his way to the sacristy to dress for mass. Father Donovan gave him a surprised greeting and asked about Johnny Bates. David gave the priest a quick explanation and asked about any special things to be aware of in the morning's service. Father Donovan said that they would be doing an incense blessing of the crèche right after today's sermon but there was nothing else beyond the normal celebration of the mass. David was familiar with handling the incense burner and gave Father Donovan a quick nod of understanding and acknowledgment.

As promised by Father Donovan, the mass proceeded as normal, without anything out of the ordinary. David fulfilled his part, although he did not really relish serving with Ronnie Hovett. As the sermon was delivered, the altar servers were always somewhat relieved, as this was the only time during the service that they could sit down; the rest of their time they were either standing or kneeling, so a long sermon was just fine with David and Ronnie. They also had a side view of the congregation, so they could eyeball the parishioners if the sermon got too boring or long, or both.

As the sermon concluded, Father Donovan gave the boys an eye signal, consisting of a raised eyebrow and head nod, that let them know to get the incense burner or Thurible, its official name, going with the charcoal starter so that the incense would burn as required for the blessing of the crèche. Although not the best of companions, Ronnie and David worked well enough together to get the required equipment ready and going for Father Donovan. Like two well-trained soldiers, they carried out the mission as instructed.

The priest filled the burner with incense and swung it slowly on the chain attached to the top of the Thurible to help get air circulating in it and assist in the burn rate. The priest first turned the incense toward the altar and then the three of them bowed to the altar and turned to parade toward the crèche. The manger scene was set up on one side of the communion rail with the scene facing the congregation and away from the altar, so the celebrant priest and his altar boy attendants could not see the crèche until they left the altar sanctuary and made their way around in front of the communion rail.

David actually liked the smell of the incense, so this was one ritual that he enjoyed. The troupe made their way to face the holy family, shepherds, kings, and barn animals. David held the incense burner with his right hand, being careful to only grab the chain ring at the top to ensure that he did not burn his hands, and he held the length of hang chain in his left hand at the ready to hand off to Father Donovan at the appropriate moment. As they were making their way into position, he scanned the congregation for the Edmonds family and made quick eye contact with his mom, who was, of course, smiling proudly at her son. Once aligned with the crèche, David kept his gaze on the incense burner to ensure that he did not burn himself, set his cassock on fire, or otherwise cause some kind of major misstep before handing things off to Father Donovan. On cue, the priest turned to David and took the incense burner into his grasp so that he could swing it toward the manger scene while pronouncing the blessing. The swinging was not only ceremonial but ensured that additional airflow would pass through the Thurible device and it would cooperatively emit the requisite smoke. As the priest took charge of the burner and David released it to him, David looked at the crèche scene for the first time. His gaze instinctively was drawn to the Christ child in the manger but it only took a second for his brain to quickly recognize the rainbow-colored tunic, the robe underneath, the scruffy beard, and the long hair. David had to step back as the power of the now-familiar scene started to buckle his knees. He was quickly enveloped in staring at the man and lost any connection with the mass, the blessing, Father Donovan, and the entire congregation.

This was the man, all right, but somehow not the man. It was a statue, but it was unmistakably the same image that David had seen before. The clothes, beard, and hair were the same, and although the face was turned away from him, he could tell it held a striking likeness to his ghostly vision. David could only stare and study the statue as Father Donovan went about his ceremonial chores. David tried to stretch his head around farther to better see the face on the statue and make some sense out of this latest encounter. He scanned the statue up and down, taking in every detail that he could and trying to connect these with the bits of memory in his mind from his previous encounters. As he studied the motionless image, he realized that he had not really had much of a chance to study the man previously and wondered if this similar-looking statue was just a weird coincidence. He was sure the tunic and wrap were identical to what he had seen previously, and the beard and hair also seemed to be a reasonable match to his previous encounters. He could not help but feel convinced that he was indeed facing what appeared to be a different incarnation of the man. As he continued to study it, he noticed the bare feet in the humble sandals. He could not really remember seeing the feet of the man previously. Something about the simple sandals with a single strap across the metatarsal part of the foot seemed familiar, but he could not be sure. He also had to consider the embarrassing encounter with the person on the street in Spokane who was not the man. Could this just be another misidentification? The loneliness of being the only one caught in this dilemma haunted him again. Even though he had taken Becky into his confidence, he knew that she could not really share in the actual experience.

The ceremonial blessing was first for the crèche and then the procedure was to turn and bless the congregation. The priest would generally just rotate to face the pews and then stroll down the center aisle spreading incense smoke and his heavenly blessing on the faithful. When the time came to perform the congregation blessing, the celebrant and Ronnie Hovett did the expected and well-practiced pivot to face the waiting congregation. David, however, did not make the rotation but instead continued to study the familiar but now-porcelain figure in the manger scene. Father Donovan was accustomed to servers being absent-minded and missing cues during the service, so he did not react immediately to David's inaction and seemingly frozen demeanor. He waited patiently for David to snap to life and follow the lead of Ronnie and himself. Unfortunately, as the seconds ticked by, to Father Donovan it seemed as if David had morphed into a statue himself.

"David, pssst! David." Father Donovan whispered to the immobile David. Father Donovan was trying to keep his voice projected toward David and away from the pews of staring faithful but to be loud enough to penetrate David's trance. David did not move or change his gaze away from the statue in the humble stable scene. The priest was now staring at David trying to determine what was going on with him. Father Donovan gave David another verbal prompt, this time with a little bit higher volume, but the result was the same.

Father Donovan was now both puzzled and irritated. He reached out to nudge David on the arm to try to get his attention away from the manger. As he made contact, David took a step back and swung his gaze toward Father Donovan, but it was a gaze without content. His eyes were glazed and not really seeing the priest right in front of him. David continued to look the priest but still with no recognition. The priest was flummoxed about this behavior, as he had not really seen behavior anything quite like this, at least not in his recent memory. He made another whispered plea to David to try to break into his glazed-over eyes. David finally woke up to current reality, and although he continued to stare into the priest eyes, it was now with recognition and the clear synchronization of being in the present moment.

"Sorry, Father," David whispered as he squeezed in another look back at the familiar figure in the stable. David fixed his gaze on the figure for a few seconds longer and then turned to continue with the blessing of the congregation. The priest studied his normally reliable server for a second longer and then decided that the congregation could not wait any longer for the ceremonial spreading of the holy incense smoke.

David did the requisite mechanical motions to complete the stroll through the church but made sure he did not make eye contact with his family, especially his mother, as she would have certainly noticed the clumsy stop at the manger and the priestly nudging required to get him moving.

The mass finished without further incident, except that David kept slanting his gaze back toward the manger, even though it was facing away from him and he no longer could see into it or the all-too-familiar menacing figure. After mass ended, he put away his cassock and surplice and felt he had to return to the crèche to make sure of what he thought he saw there. He knew this would be unusual, as the servers always exited the sacristy through an outside door.

"David, are you all right today? I was worried during the blessing when you seemed to be completely distant and in some sort of hypnotic state or something." Father Donovan's unexpected quizzing interrupted David's thought of making his way back to the crèche. David turned to Father Donovan and stuttered a response that seemed to satisfy the priest, or at least cut off any further questions, which was enough for David. Father Donovan cocked his head with his eyes bearing in on David as if to extract more information by virtue of his glare. With one eye open slightly more than the other, he studied David's facial expression in a vain attempt to better understand.

But then the priest shrugged, nodded, and looked away. He was more than willing to surrender any further concern or tacit responsibility for the boy's strange behavior to his parents, friends, or anyone else around.

David nervously fiddled with cleaning some of the instruments from the mass in an effort to buy some time for the priest to lose interest in his odd behavior and give him time to exit through the church and back to the manger scene without inciting more curious suspicion from the priest. Generally, the servers did not do the cleaning of the chalices and such, so David's feigning of cleaning was itself a bit suspicious. Ronnie Hovett had already disrobed and dashed out the side exit to join his family, so David's delay was out of place from the norm.

David started to realize that Father Donovan would remain in the sacristy longer than he could continue his contrived delay. He decided he needed a different course of action to get back to the manger without arousing even more suspicion from Father Donovan. He decided to just shoot out a hastily conjured reason and go with it.

"Father, I'm going to exit through the church since my folks are probably parked right out front anyway so that would the shortest way and anyway would probably be less icy and safer. I hope you have a good Sunday."

"OK, David. Say hello to your mom and dad." Father Donovan responded in spontaneous reaction without really having given any thought to the unusual and actually ridiculous reasoning being given by David for this type of exit.

David did not wait for the priest to analyze and question such logic but made a quick exit into the sanctuary and around the altar, where he gave a well-practiced but less than devout genuflection. As he exited through the communion rail and turned left toward the manger scene, his heart started to race and sweat started to bubble in his armpits.

His pace was quick but apprehensive as he approached the holy scene.

Sure enough, as he stood in front of the manger, the man was there just as he had seen during the mass. David positioned himself so he could better see the man's face and to David's dread it, too, was a disturbingly close facsimile of the man. The expression, however, was not the same as what David had seen before. The statue had the expression of wonder. Of course, that is what you would expect to be portrayed in such a scene of people witnessing the birth of Christ.

David struggled to make sense of the statue and its obvious likeness to the mysterious man. How can this statue and his hallucinations be the same? Was his mind somehow conjuring up this guy from memories of this statue? He realized he had not really paid much attention to the manger scene itself and where this figure fit into the Christmas cast. He stepped back to get a broader view of the scene, and it was easy to see that "his" guy was really Saint Joseph. He studied it more to make sure he was not misinterpreting things. He tried to think back to his religion classes to see if he could recall anything that might explain why Saint Joseph would be tormenting him. He could not gather all the raging thoughts and turbulent theories in his head and he was starting to feel a dizziness overtake him.

"David, what are you doing? We have been waiting in the car for almost twenty minutes!" Paul Edmonds's voice was stern and scolding in tone.

David spun around to see his dad staring at him from the center aisle of the church. The expression on Paul Edmonds's face told David that he had pushed his dad a bit too far this morning.

"Dad, I was just checking everything to make sure all the things got put away correctly."

"C'mon, son, we are all waiting on you in the cold with the car running out here. Not to mention some of us would like to have some breakfast this morning."

David quickly turned and sheepishly made his way to the center aisle where his dad was waiting for him. He gave a swift glance at his dad's face to try to gauge the level of disappointment there. What he saw told him that Paul Edmonds was not amused by this unexplained delay, and so David quickly shifted his gaze toward the floor and joined his dad for the walk toward the back of the church. David could not help but give a glance back toward the crèche as he approached the rear exit. As his vision caught focus of the manger scene, he saw that the Saint Joseph statue had turned its head and was looking toward the congregation, and him, and no longer at the Christ child as before! David stopped in his tracks to fix his eyes on the statue but as he did so he lost focus momentarily. When he refocused on the statue, it was clearly looking at the child again. David remained stopped and continued to watch the manger scene while his dad continued the walk toward the exit, at least until Paul Edmonds realized that David had stopped again.

"Now what?" Paul barked at David in a voice that had lost not only patience but the reverence one normally maintains when speaking in a church.

David shook his head and turned toward his dad. He didn't verbally respond, he just kept walking. Had the statue been looking at him? This latest event was not just another weird encounter; this was a statue, for heaven's sake, and it was a dead ringer for his apparition. David walked out of the church and to the car in silence, but his mind was anything but silent as it raced with trying to hatch some kind of rationalization of this latest experience.

The ride home was mostly nonverbal, but David could sense his parents' concern for him and his strange behavior. Paul Edmonds's facial cue to David's mom was a clear signal not to bring anything up about what had happened at mass with David and to keep things silent for now. So it was a long and quiet ride home from church for David, although his younger siblings bubbled with talk of Christmas and anticipation for the hearty Sunday morning breakfast they always treasured.

As the Buick made its way out of town and back to the familiar confines of the Edmonds dairy, David kept thinking of Becky. He longed to tell her about the statue and its uncanny resemblance to his troubling man. He felt sure talking to Becky would give him a better sense of whether this was reality, or just his reality. For the first time since he had seen her last night, he felt completely at ease with having shared his story with her. It was like a pressure relief value that he needed to make sure his trauma did not overwhelm him. David had been comfortable with Becky the evening before, but now he was able to really relax with his decision to confide in her about his experiences with the ghostly specter. He began to conjure in his mind what he would say to her about the experience with the statue at church. He knew he would have to include explanations regarding the Catholic rituals because Becky and her family were practicing Presbyterians and, like most Protestants, Becky found the Catholic Church rituals to be odd and foreign.

David made a silent trek directly to his bedroom once they arrived at home. He flopped facedown on the bed and let his emotions float out of his ransacked brain, at least for a moment. He ran the events backwards from this morning to the first time he had encountered the man, or Saint Joseph, or whoever he was supposed to be. He tried to look for some relevant detail that might somehow explain what was happening to him. He did not really know what he was looking for, but he was hopeful he could fetch something meaningful to assist in his search for an answer. As David let his mind float, his thoughts drifted toward that shiny 1955 Chevy Bel Air he still was longing for this Christmas. Thoughts of the Chevy helped take his mind off the past week's events. He hoped for a 1955 Chevy that was two-tone baby blue and white. He was sure his dad would understand his desire for a car, but he wasn't as sure about his mom. She was on the fence about it and he knew she would have veto authority in the end. He had his eye on such a Chevy at the local dealer, although it was two-tone red and white, but that was close enough for David. Now the question was would his dad apply the proper amount of persuasion to his mom to make it happen. He knew they probably would not tip their hand, and he would have to wait until the big day.

In his mind, he envisioned the dashboard, the backseat, the engine, and even the trunk space. He thought about Becky sitting next to him as he cruised Main Street and smiled as he passed his buddies. This mental image had a smiling Becky with her left hand cautiously but flirtatiously resting on David's thigh.

"David, may we speak for a moment?" Janet Edmonds's sharp but motherly voice cut into the dreamy Chevy ride with Becky and gave David a start.

"Uh, sure, Mom. Come in," David replied as he quickly rolled over and made eye contact with his mom.

"David, I want to know what happened at mass today. You looked like you really had some kind of a problem during the blessing. Are you all right?"

David stuttered and stammered as he did some quick mental and verbal gymnastics to allay his mom's concerns about the strange behavior at church. Although David felt his storyline was solid, to Janet Edmonds it was a tepid story at best.

"David, this is similar to the strange thing that happened at the basketball game the other night. Is there some connection?"

"Mom, it's nothing really. I'm fine. Maybe just a little stressed about Christmas or something."

Mrs. Edmonds's raised eyebrows and pursed lips made it clear she didn't buy David's porous storyline, but she needed to get Sunday morning breakfast started, so she accepted it and got back to her duties in the kitchen. Janet Edmonds knew that part of her motherly duty was to make sure she at least stuck her nose into her children's business. She felt she had accomplished that much. David blew out a sigh of relief as his mom left his room, and he rolled back over with his face and his guilt of lying to his mom pressed into the crumpled bed sheets.

David forced himself to partake in the normal chatty breakfast conversation, although his appetite was not with him this morning. As soon as the breakfast chores were complete, David called Becky to confirm that she could meet with him later today.

They met in the afternoon and discussed the latest events of that morning at mass. Becky listened intently as David poured out the details of the unsettling experience with the statue. When he finished, Becky remained silent and pensive as she mulled this statue situation over in her mind. She was troubled that her beau might really be experiencing some sort of mental breakdown and losing his connection with reality. She knew him well enough to know that this was very out of character for David Edmonds, who was usually very grounded in the here and now, his daydreaming notwithstanding.

"David, you said the statue was looking at you when you and your dad were leaving the church?" Becky broke the silence.

"Yes, well, I think so. You see, I was facing away from the manger scene as we walked out and when I glanced back, I could swear that the Saint Joseph statue had turned its head and was looking at me."

"But then couldn't your dad have seen it also?"

"Well, of course, but the shock of seeing this caused me to stop and look again. This time the statue was as before, just looking at the Christ child."

"Hmm," Becky purred as she thought about this while staring out the windshield of David's parents' Buick, which he had managed to commandeer for this rendezvous in spite of the slide into the snowbank last night.

David also remained silent for the moment and let their thoughts mingle and ferment. He started to feel a little unsettled now with having told Becky so much of what had happened. He could feel in her demeanor a certain level of doubt about his sanity or maybe even his honesty. He was certain that Becky did not think him dishonest, but he did not really know how to read her. He almost felt like he was sitting next to a stranger instead of his steady girl, and it gave him a chill.

Becky again broke the silence. "I think maybe with all that you have experienced, you just thought you saw the statue looking at you but in reality it was unchanged. Doesn't that seem more plausible?"

"Maybe, but I swear that thing was looking at me." David pondered Becky's comment but as his mind's eye re-created the scene, he again could plainly see the face of the statue, the man, looking at him as he glanced back that morning. "In fact, I can still see it, Becky. It was looking right at me. I know it seems crazy, but I don't know what else to think about it."

"David, you know I believe you saw what you saw. I just want to make sure that you consider every possibility."

"Including that I'm losing my mind?" David shot back and regretted his thoughtless retort as soon as it left his tongue. "Sorry, Becky, that wasn't fair."

"I understand the stress you're under. No harm done." Becky gave him a soft love squeeze on the arm to calm them both and reassure him of her feelings for him.

They continued to chat about what had been happening and mentally thumbing through the sequence of strange sightings one by one and day by day. In the end, they could not come up with any real conclusions. They both were struck with what this possible connection to Saint Joseph could mean or whether it was just a really strange coincidence.

Although she did not feel it was the time to voice it, Becky couldn't help but wonder if the statue, which had been used in the Catholic Church in Seltice Falls as part of Christmas for as long as anyone could remember, had triggered the visions in the first place. Maybe this was some kind of reverse association that David's subconscious had formed into a version of reality. That seemed a reasonable explanation, although it did not explain why David's mind would have resorted to this paranormal activity in the first place. Becky thought about the ritualistic activities that she had observed of the Catholic Church and how the church revered statues and objects. This was very different from her religious experience in the Presbyterian ranks, where the focus was on the scripture and not on rituals and objects. The more she thought about it, the more logical it became. David's exposure and his own pious upbringing could possibly have triggered a manifestation of the statue in David's mind. As these "rational" explanations matured in her mind, she drew comfort in them. It helped to think that David's sightings could logically be attributed to his influence from the church and not anything to do with him losing his sanity. Admittedly this theory overlooked the simple fact that having these illusions was still far from anything normal, Catholic or not, but Becky was undeterred. She secured herself to this line of logic as a way to rest her mind about what was happening to her dear David. They both let the silence settle between them as they snuggled together in the front seat of the Buick with the radio serenading them with some familiar Christmas music. The silence gave them both a chance to envelop themselves in the moment and to let the stress of the mysterious man evaporate, at least for now.

Their conversation reignited after a while, but on a new track, as they started to speak about Christmas and what they would be doing over the next week with no school. Becky told David she would be spending time with her extended family and seeing her favorite uncle Dan, who so reminded her of her late father. For Becky this made the holidays both troublesome and joyous. She dearly missed her dad, but she also enjoyed experiencing him virtually through the familiar connections of his family. David talked about the car he was sure his parents were planning on getting him this Christmas. Since he did not really know what car he was going to get, he could not describe it physically, but he had an uncanny ability to paint the mental experience of driving it and taking Becky for a ride. He even spoke of some of the things he would do to "fix it up."

As the day started to fade toward late afternoon, they embraced again and closed their time with a passionate kiss that never lasted long enough for Becky.

"I need to get home. I have about fifty cows that are waiting for me," David said as he parted from her soft and affectionate lips.

"I know, I know. You dairy farmers! That is one thing I do not want to do when I grow up." Becky's words were a statement of her desire but her eyes searched David's countenance to see if he thought his future would include dairy cows. She had envisioned them together in marriage more than once and wanted to provide some guidance on how she foresaw the future.

David did not respond regarding the cows but instead just laughed at Becky's irritation concerning the management of a modern dairy. He steered the Buick back onto the road and toward Becky's home. They had parked near the vacant and snow-covered City Park, where there was not a soul in sight. As they drove the lonely city street, the frozen snow crunched under the weight of the slow-moving car.

David let his eyes roam the short horizon in front of them until his view came to rest on the one thing he did not want to see. There was no mistaking it, and David hit the brakes hard, sending the car into a skid once again. Standing on the sidewalk between two leafless maple trees was the man.

"**M**y God, there he is!" David shouted as the careening Buick continued to slide down the ice-coated asphalt.

"David!" was all Becky could say as her eyes were locked straight forward watching the front end of the car as it slowly pivoted sideways in a slide.

Due to the slow speed that David had been traveling, the car did not skid far and came to rest quickly in the middle of the road at about a twenty-degree angle, with the nose of the car pointing toward the right side of the road. Becky had put her hands out on the dashboard in anticipation of a collision, but fortunately she didn't require that precaution. Becky's heart raced as she spun her head toward David to see why he hit the brakes. But David did not take any notice of Becky's glare; his view was frozen to the right-hand side of the road, looking between two maple tree trunks.

"David, what is it?" Becky stared at him.

"It's him . . . it's that damn man . . . or Saint Joseph!" David almost shouted but not really at Becky, as he never took his eyes from the man.

Becky finally followed his line of sight toward the maple trees. As she did, she realized she really did not want to see anything; she did not want to be part of this bizarre phenomenon. It was too late however, because her head was already in motion and brought the maple trees in view before she could persuade them otherwise. Almost to her surprise, the maple trees looked like two maple trees should look in winter, bare and cold. The snow was piled up around them from people shoveling the walkway and from the street plows. There was no person there, nothing unusual that would spark the kind of reaction that was coming from David. She scanned the walkway left to right and even looked up in the trees and the front yards of the homes along the street, but there was no sign of anyone. She turned her eyes back toward David, who was still transfixed in the same immobile stare between the two maple trees. She pivoted her head several times, following David's line of sight back and forth to make sure she was not missing something, or maybe someone. But there was nothing there.

"He's right there staring at us!" David sounded frightened this time.

"OK, David." But Becky kept her vision fixed on David's eyes, his facial expression, and his body language.

David watched as the man once again had a look of dissatisfaction on his face and once again spread his arms and looked skyward. David wanted to get out of the car and chase him down, but he found himself unable to move. The man had the same clothes as before, a simple tunic and robe with those rainbow colors he had seen on the statue. As he studied him, he remembered about the sandals he had seen on the statue. Sure enough the man had what looked like identical footwear. David was convinced now that there was some kind of a connection between the man and the Saint Joseph figure in the nativity scene at church. The man lowered his arms and head and once again gave David a scolding look. He then turned and walked toward the maple tree on the left. As he passed behind the large and stately tree trunk, he seemed to disappear.

David suddenly found functionality in his limbs. He quickly opened the door and jumped from the car in pursuit. Becky almost fell over from his fast departure, as she had still been leaning on him. The blast of cold from the outside gave her a start as well. She stepped from the car but did not pursue David. Instead she stood in the street holding onto the driver's door and watching him. David raced to the left maple tree and dashed around it in an attempt to catch the ghostly man. Of course, there was no one there when David rounded the tree trunk, only the tracks that stopped impossibly in the snow where the man had vanished.

He had seen these footprints before, of course, yesterday morning when he had pursued the man through the snow and fog. He remembered the odd flat footprint, not like what a winter boot or shoe would leave in the snow. It was the sandals all along, something that would have been worn at the time of the first Christmas. David concluded that this must connect somehow with the statue or Saint Joseph, but how and why was he having this experience? Wouldn't it make more sense for a holier person to have these visions, like a priest or pastor?

David followed the tracks back to where the man had been standing. As he suspected, the tracks started there. Again, an impossibility unless the man could fly. David almost chuckled at this thought, but nothing else made any sense. He studied the tracks for some time and then had a thought.

"Becky, come over here, please."

She closed the door on the still-idling car that was mostly blocking the right lane of the street. She looked around and saw there wasn't any traffic, and even though it made her uncomfortable to leave the car sitting like that, she decided it was not a major concern. She walked briskly to where David was standing between the two maple trees.

David looked straight into her frightened eyes. "You didn't see him, did you?"

"No, I didn't."

"Don't worry about it. Take a look here. What do you see?" David stepped back from the footprints trying to be as objective as possible in soliciting her analysis.

Becky stepped forward and studied the snow-covered ground where David had indicated. She spent some time looking at it to make sure she was capturing everything.

"Do you mean those strange footprints in the snow right there?" Becky was pointing right at the guilty footprints as she looked up at David.

"Yes, those strange footprints, right there. You know why they are strange?" David continued without waiting for an answer. "Because they are made by someone wearing sandals. The man, Becky, the man."

Becky studied the snow and could see a flat, featureless outline that was clearly in the shape of the sole of a strange shoe. As David said, the print was not from a typical winter boot. A winter-soled boot would have left cleat marks. It was also not a print that would have been made by a dress shoe, as there was no heel impression. As she continued to study the marks, she followed their trail just to the maple tree, where they stopped. The snow was only a day old and because it had remained cold, the prints from the previous day had filled with some of the later-day snow or were somewhat crusted over and aged. These prints were not like that. They looked as fresh as the prints that Becky's own footsteps now imparted to the snow.

"You see them, don't you?" David could discern from watching Becky's study of the ground that she could see the strange prints. He felt a wave of satisfaction or maybe just raw relief that someone else was also being drawn into this mystery. "You can see that they are just like you might leave if you were wearing a simple sandal from the time of Christ."

"David, that is just too weird. What do you mean a sandal from the time of Christ? This is the 1960s and we are in Northern Idaho." Becky was shaking from either the cold or the experience, she wasn't sure which.

"Don't you see? The man is dressed like someone from that time period. I made sure to look for that this time when I saw him. He was wearing simple sandals, Becky. Those sandals made those marks in the snow."

"David, this just can't be. I mean, that is just crazy and you are scaring me now."

"Did you think I was just making all this up? Don't you think that I'm scared, too? Becky, think about it. Somehow this thing that I'm seeing must be real or at least not just in my mind. You were here and you know that I didn't make those prints and neither did anyone else on this deserted street.

A car slowly rolled up from the opposite direction and the driver rolled down the window as it came to a stop in the street.

"Are you kids OK?" It was Mr. Monroe, who ran the local hardware and farm supply store in town. He had always been a good friend of the Edmondses, as they were always good customers and friends.

"Hi, Mr. Monroe. Yes, we are fine. We thought we saw a lost cat we were looking for and had to stop right away," David lied.

With a wave and smile, Mr. Monroe slowly moved along and edged past the idling, awkwardly parked Buick. David and Becky exchanged looks. Becky had never known David to lie about anything, but she knew immediately that she would have to condone this one, at least for the moment.

"Let's get back in the car" Becky said and turned to walk toward it.

David studied the prints a bit longer but then joined her. He put the car in gear and moved it slowly to the edge of the street where he parked it but left the motor running, mostly to keep the heater going so they could both thaw out from the cold and the latest shared encounter with the unique snow prints.

Becky and David sat quietly in the car for several minutes, neither of them wanting to broach the subject of the man. Becky could only snuggle closer to David. She now felt a deeper connection to him because of their shared experience. Becky had thus far convinced herself that this entire experience was somehow exclusive to David's imagination or mind or something unique to him. She had always felt strongly that David was being completely honest in what he *thought* he was experiencing, but Becky had never really thought that this was something that was happening in the physical world. Now she found that she had to confront the frightening prospect of these events being something not only otherworldly but now squarely in her world, the real world. She had not really prepared herself for this reality, and she shivered as she pondered it. Her mind was racing and scared because even if the prints were of this world, they clearly started and stopped right where David indicated the man's presence.

"David, I'm scared. How can some kind of specter be haunting both of us? I wonder why I did not see him if I can see the footprints?" Becky was speaking almost to herself as much as David as she continued to look out the window at the snow-covered sidewalk.

"I wish I knew. I don't have any idea what this guy is all about, and no one can see him but me. I have to admit that I find some comfort in the fact that at least you saw the footprints." David spoke while also continuing to look out the car window at the last vanishing point of the man.

"I'm sure you do, but I don't find any comfort in any of this. What are we going to do?" Becky pleaded.

"We're going to keep this between the two of us until we can figure it out. No one is going to believe us anyway, and it will just cause a big uproar. I mean even your mom, Becky. We can't tell anyone about it."

"Don't worry, I don't plan on saying anything to anyone, but how do we figure it out? It's so random."

"I don't know yet, but let me think about it tonight, OK?" David pleaded as Becky turned her eyes, now moist with tears, toward David for some solace. He hugged her tighter.

They solidified their mutual code of silence regarding the strange man. David dropped Becky off at home, albeit later than anticipated by her mom.

"Becky, you were supposed to be home an hour ago. What happened?" Mary Marston quizzed Becky as soon as she arrived at home.

"Sorry, Mom. I guess time just got away from us. We like to talk a lot about things."

"Talk a lot? That doesn't sound like most seventeen-year-old boys that I knew." Her mom scoffed but with a subtle smile.

"David is different. We talk about the future and things at school, you know."

Becky spent some time chatting with her mom and then made her way to her bedroom, where she sprawled on the bed staring at the ceiling and wondering about what she had witnessed, while at the same time trying to mentally move it out of the macabre and into the normal reality of Seltice Falls. With this she was not successful. No amount of mental gymnastics could make sense of it. The footprints were burned into her memory, and she could not shake the images from her mind. She finally got up, undressed, put on her nightgown, brushed her teeth, and snuggled under the welcoming quilts on her bed. She spent a troubled hour tossing and turning before exhaustion provided some peaceful sleep.

David hurried to the milk parlor as soon as he got home, as he knew the milking process was well under way.

"Nice you could show up," Paul Edmonds fired at David when he popped into the milking pit where his dad was already working.

"Sorry, Dad," was all David could muster, but it seemed enough. Paul Edmonds knew enough about young people and their relationships not to be too surprised at his son's tardiness. Little did he realize the true reason behind David's reason for being late.

David kept his focus on the milking procedure, but his mind continued to study the mental images from this afternoon. He had renewed confidence in himself now that Becky had also seen the footprints. He could not conjure up a reason for her being able to see the prints only and not the man himself, but he was comforted still by the fact that Becky was now a true partner in this truly bizarre experience. He tried to put together all the different elements, the first appearance, right here in the milking parlor, the strange appearance at the basketball game, the sighting in the fog of the early morning, the vision in front of the car, then the strange occurrence with the statue in the church, and now this afternoon. What was the connection between these events? Why were these visions happening at all? Was it something that David did in his past, or was it something that he needed to do now, or maybe in the future? David mulled this around as he worked through the motions in the dairy barn, but he could not get his mind to narrow in on a common theme or final answer to any of it.

After chores, David wanted to call Becky again, but he decided that this would be a bit too much for Becky's mom and would probably start to raise some kind of suspicion with her. So instead, David retired to his bedroom, where he lay on his bed and pondered his next move, how to solve this puzzle. As events and theories traversed through his brain, he tried to zero in on something to unravel things, a key or cipher. His mind became exhausted with this riddle and his body soon followed, which at least allowed him to drift into a deep sleep.

David rose early as always to work the never-ending chores that are part of the dairy farm life. Cows were not really on his mind as he efficiently went through the motions. His dad helped him for the final portion of the herd and noticed that David was pensive this morning and not his usual chatty self. Paul Edmonds was not one to pry too much into someone else's business, so he kept his observations to himself as they both finished cleaning the equipment and parlor.

Breakfast was more festive than usual as this was December 24. Janet Edmonds had prepared a large meal that rivaled the normal Sunday fare, and everyone except David ate heartily and quickly. David ate slowly and even seemed to pick at his food, which was very unusual for him. He was usually the last one to quit eating and was almost always out to ensure no leftovers remained. He kept thinking about what he could do to try to unravel and understand this situation. It had taken on a renewed sense of purpose and energy since Becky had been reluctantly pulled into his dilemma via the strange footprints in the snow yesterday. He kept rolling over in his mind a way to figure out what was happening. He was keen on math, science, and logic in general, and this seemed the best way to think about it. He just wasn't sure where to start. Finding that first piece of the puzzle to work with had been on his mind all morning. He needed a thread to give him some direction.

Suddenly it hit him. "Of course!" He blurted out as he stared at his half-full plate of food.

"What are you talking about?" his sister Katy shot back with an irritated and quizzical look on her face. "Are you on the same planet as the rest of us?" She continued with a laugh, now clearly amused at her older brother's sudden departure from normal breakfast table behavior.

David looked up at the faces around the table, all of which were now focused on him. It was as if he was seeing them for the first time this morning, and he suddenly felt like he had just been dropped into the present.

"Uh, oh, nothing, you guys, just something at school that I have been working on and I just thought of a solution." David's response was tentative at best, but he felt it should suffice. "Well, not a complete solution maybe but some ideas about it."

"Well, David, I think you should provide us a bit more of an explanation about this school problem now that you have all of our attention." Janet Edmonds was trying to find out what was going on with her son. She knew it was unlikely a kid worried about school while on Christmas break and on December 24.

Katy could not resist a sibling missile across the table. "Probably more about Becky Marston than anything at school!"

David just ignored her. "Mom, it's nothing really, just a problem in class that we were all working on, and an idea just struck me about it."

"OK, but I want to know more when you complete the project."

"Sure, Mom, of course, and it doesn't have anything to do with Becky." David then asked to be excused and if he could borrow the car for a while. Janet was not too keen on this as it was the day before Christmas and she had lots of last-minute things to do. Paul Edmonds came through for David, though, and let him use the old Ford pickup truck. David said he would try to not be late.

"You had better not be late. Tonight is Christmas Eve, David Edmonds" his mom reminded him in more of a scold than anything.

David reassured her he would be home in time for everything, including milking the cows. After changing his clothes, he bounded out to the pickup truck to head into town.

David's epiphany was the connection with Saint Joseph. He realized that this was the thread he needed to try to tie things together. He headed toward the church to confront the statue. With everyone preparing the church for Christmas Eve, he felt confident that the sanctuary would be unlocked and he could enter without drawing any undue suspicion.

Besides revisiting the church, he was planning on a stop at the local library to do some research on this little-known saint. He hoped studying the scripture might provide him a clue that would connect back to him and his small life here in Seltice Falls. This all seemed like a long shot, but at least it was a thread he could pursue.

As he hoped, the church was open and several of the church ladies were working inside to finalize Christmas decorations for the midnight mass later. He knew them all and said a cordial and quiet hello as he entered the sanctuary. He spent some time in the pew in prayer, at least feigned prayer. The women recognized David as "that nice Edmonds boy." They were polite and did not question him being in the church. They knew he was an altar server and assumed he was there to prepare for the service.

David finished his "prayer" time in the pew and made his way up to the manger scene near the front of the church. He knelt in front of it as if in prayer so as not to draw too much attention to himself from the women. He made sure his position gave him the best unobstructed view of the Saint Joseph statue. He fixed his gaze on it as if in a trance. He studied the hair, the beard, the tunic, and the blanket cover. He especially studied the sandals. They were just as he remembered and exactly what would leave the kind of footprints in snow that he saw that day in the fog and yesterday with Becky. He still could not understand how this statue and the man could be the same, but there was no denying the physical likeness. The appearances were too close to be just a coincidence. The face of the statue was poised to view the Christ child in the manger. David craned his neck to try to look into the eyes of the statue, but the angle was not conducive to this view. As he stared at the face of the statue, his focus was so intense that he almost expected the statue's head to turn and look at him. But the head did not budge; it stayed stationary and immobile. David held his gaze but to no avail. There was no movement from the porcelain Saint Joseph image.

David finally decided that he was not going to get the enlightenment he was hoping for at church today, so he slowly got up and retreated to the center aisle of the church, where he genuflected and made his way out. He decided not to make a last look back at the crèche this time as he exited the church. He headed to his next stop, the Seltice Falls Public Library.

Fortunately for David, the library was open today. Not surprisingly, the library was all but abandoned except for one lonely librarian manning the checkout and multipurpose desk at the foyer entrance. David knew Mrs. Cummings, of course, because she had been a fixture at the library desk for as long as he could remember.

"Good morning, David. Nice to see you, and Merry Christmas. What brings you into the library on the day before Christmas?" Mrs. Cummings greeted David.

"Good morning, Mrs. Cummings, and a Merry Christmas to you. I see I will have the place to myself today," David responded with a smile and chuckle. "Not too often you see a high schooler here on a day like this, I guess. Well, for me, I'm doing some research that can't really wait so . . . here I am."

"I hope you find what you're looking for. Let me know if you need help with it. I could use something more interesting to do than filing books back on the shelf."

"Well, I actually need to find some biblical research material on Saint Joseph." David realized he could probably use all the help he could muster and did not think Mrs. Cummings would find the subject matter suspicious. Unfortunately, he caught Mrs. Cummings off guard.

"Saint Joseph? I would think Mickey Mantle or Paul Horning, or maybe even Santa Claus would be more likely for a boy your age?" Her tone had that nervous hint of suspicion that gave David a twist of the gut, and he found himself searching for some plausible reason why he would want to research some enigmatic figure like Saint Joseph.

Being the day before Christmas was now working to his advantage and allowed him to reply without too much hesitation.

"Good question," David responded with a nervous chuckle. "Actually, it's part of a church project that I need for the service tomorrow."

"Oh, I guess that makes sense. You can find the biblical reference materials over on aisle three near the middle on the right-hand side. Is there something specific that I can help you find?" Mrs. Cummings was being a bit too tenacious for David's liking, so he needed to circumvent any more help.

"No, not just yet. I need to do some general research to start." With that, David turned and headed straight toward aisle three.

The library was built before the war but had been remodeled in 1955, so although it was not palatial or scholarly like one of the Carnegie libraries, it was practical and efficient. The library was small and cozy, with the inviting smell of books and that atmosphere of quiet comfort that embodies libraries. David had been here often when he was younger, but the high school had its own library, so the need to visit the town library had diminished.

David scanned the bookshelves to try to get his bearings. Being Catholic, he was not as familiar with the bible as Becky would be, as the Catholic Church relied more on its catechism for the indoctrination of its youth, whereas

97

Becky's Presbyterian ministry was based more on the direct reading of the King James Bible.

David decided his best place to start would be the bible. He figured it would be the best opportunity to connect the Saint Joseph experience to this man from two thousand years ago. He scanned the shelves and found a Catholic bible published by The Catholic Press. He wasn't sure why, but he decided to start with this version. Probably the fact that it was Catholic gave it more of a home field advantage for his search. It was a large, elegant book with reference tabs and ornate illustrations. The illustrations were of interest to David because his experience to this point had all been visual. This would allow him to search for an illustration of his mystery man.

David noticed the illustrations in this version of the bible were all taken from paintings by James Tissot. Tissot was a nineteenth-century French artist. David had learned in an art class that Tissot was not originally a strong Christian but then the death of a women friend turned his thoughts more to matters of the soul. He joined the Catholic Church, and during a trip to Palestine in 1886, he focused his work on sketching the stories from the bible. His work was noteworthy and recognized for its authenticity and allegiance to the bible story, as well as the landscapes and geography of the habitat of where Jesus walked.

David splayed the book onto the nearest table, planted himself into a chair, and began to scan the index so that he could focus on narrowing this intimidating draft of God's word on his mental prey.

David decided that the Christmas story was the best place to start his search. He knew that he needed to look at either the book of Matthew or Luke for the Christmas story because the books of Mark and John did not include the familiar stories of the birth of Christ.

He thumbed through to Luke, which has the most detailed story of the first Christmas. He read chapter 2, verses 1–53. Joseph had protected his family on their journey to Bethlehem, as well as provided a stable home in Nazareth. Joseph's stability as a father also showed through when Jesus, as a youth, had stayed behind preaching in the temple in Jerusalem, causing his parents a great deal of concern.

The book of Matthew, chapter 1, verses 18–25, spoke of the betrothal of Mary to Joseph and him being an honorable man. When he learned of Mary's pregnancy via the Holy Spirit, he was willing to break off the engagement because he was "not wishing to expose her to reproach." Only after a visit from an angel did Joseph understand the magnitude of the child within, and he knew he must honor his commitment to Mary. Matthew, chapter 2, speaks of how Joseph takes his family to Egypt to escape King Herod's plans to murder all the boy babies in the Kingdom to ensure that the rumored threat of a new king, as foretold to him by the three wise men from the east, is extinguished.

David was struck by how such a small content of writings from almost two thousand years ago had mutated into what now was known as Christmas. He realized that he had never really contemplated this aspect before, and he reread it as if for the first time. He sat back in his chair and considered the Saint Joseph figure depicted in these verses. The simple verses spoke of a gentle, dedicated family man who put his family and their welfare first, above all else. David's fear of the Joseph figure was temporarily muted as he read. The bible spoke in factual, straightforward, unambiguous language that was timeless, regardless that the story and writings were almost two thousand years in the past. David wondered if maybe the vision was something not to be feared but understood. This did not help him figure out why the visions were happening, but it helped him to relax and think more about what the experience might really be all about.

He settled back into his chair and stared straight ahead as he reimagined his various encounters with the man. He closed his eyes and concentrated on his memories of the several visions to see if there might be some clue to connect the Joseph of the bible stories to his personal version of the man. He could not really find anything concrete as he overlaid the words from the bible to mental pictures in his head.

As he relaxed his eyes and his concentration, he sat forward in his chair again and started to flip the pages. He brought his attention back to the illustrations and paged to the New Testament. The first five pages of this section were of the birth and early years of Jesus. It was the illustration of the holy family's travels to and from Egypt that caused David to snap his head in a stunned jerk forward. The first and smaller of the two paintings showed Mary holding Jesus while riding on a donkey, with Joseph walking alongside as they traveled to Egypt. In the larger painting, an older Jesus was riding the donkey with a walking Mary and Joseph. There was nothing unusual about the placement of the figures, but this was not what had shaken David. It was Joseph's garments: the white robe, the colorful tunic, and the blanket thrown over his shoulder. The colors and pattern were just as David had seen on the statue and on his mystery man. This could not be just a coincidence. David had seen enough Christmas cards and various depictions of the holy family to know that Joseph is shown in many types of garments and dress; there was no standard or norm such as what he was experiencing here with the bible and the statue, as well as the mystery man. David could only continue to stare at the picture of Joseph.

"Are you finding what you need?" Mrs. Cummings's inquiry caused David to jump with a start. He had been in another self-imposed trance to the point that he had forgotten where he was and what he was supposed to be doing. "Goodness, David, I did not mean to startle you. Is everything OK?"

David turned to look at Mrs. Cummings as if to see who was speaking to him. He could not respond right away but only stared at her. He wanted to shout at her and tell her everything that he had seen and felt this past week. Of course, he did not shout; he only slumped into his chair as he looked back at the picture of Joseph, hoping it had disappeared or changed somehow. Joseph, of course, was as before and offered no solace for David and his personal dilemma.

"David, are you all right, honey?" Mrs. Cummings whispered, displaying sympathetic concern for the young man.

"I'm not sure yet," David answered meekly.

"Is there anything I can do?"

"Thank you, but no, I am fine. I don't need anything further." David looked only at the picture of Joseph as he spoke. It was almost as if he were speaking to the book instead of Mrs. Cummings.

Mrs. Cummings retreated from the table as if spurned by a wayward lover. She kept her eye on David as she slowly walked back to her desk in the empty library. She knew him well enough to be concerned about his mysterious behavior, starting with why in the world he was in the library today. She could not help but think there might be something really troubling going on with him. She did not know how to penetrate David's mysterious demeanor, so she settled back into her routine at her desk, while keeping a sharp eye in David's direction.

David's eyes welled up as his emotions started to overcome any control he held, while the experiences in his mind continued to churn. He bowed his head as if studying the bible more intently in an effort to keep his emotional burst distant from Mrs. Cummings's frequent gazes around the library. Being the only one there did not help his cause. He could not take his eyes away from the picture of Joseph, as if he almost expected the figure to turn and look at him, or maybe show that smirk expression again. The shock of seeing this picture of Joseph took some energy out of David. He struggled to continue searching the bible for answers but kept finding himself coming back to Joseph.

David was not sure how much time had passed while he sat lost in thought. He knew he had to keep searching bible text to see if he could find anything about the mysterious Joseph figure that might link him to David's visions. Joseph played a minor role in the overall bible story and was hardly mentioned in the books of Matthew or John. The simple and small amount of text dedicated to Joseph seemed critical to the Christmas story but almost inconsequential to the bible story at large. David could not find anything that made any sense regarding his experiences with the strange man. In spite of this dead end, he felt certain that the long-dead stepfather of Jesus was somehow connected to everything. He checked with Mrs. Cummings to see if he could check out the bible and take it home with him so he could continue his research on the topic, but unfortunately she informed him the library did not allow reference books to be checked out. He decided he could just as easily use the family bible at home, although it did not have the illustrations that were so troublesome.

He put the books back on their respective shelves and then spent some time looking through additional books for more reference materials on Joseph. What he found did not provide any additional information. He slowly made his way toward the library exit with a kindly good-bye to Mrs. Cummings. He climbed into the pickup and started to drive toward home but then realized he needed to take a detour to continue his research.

He approached the church slowly and decided to park around the back, where he was less likely to be seen. Although there had been ladies there earlier in the day, the church now seemed to be deserted. He was relieved to see no other cars in the parking area, and it looked like Father Donovan was either out or engaged in something inside the parsonage.

The old pickup came to a slow stop on the crunching snow, and David slid out as quietly as possible. He made his way to the sacristy back door, which he figured would be unlocked, but he knew where the key was hidden anyway. The hidden key allowed mass servers to arrive early when required. David found the door was locked but found the hidden key with no issues. He quickly slinked inside the building, through the sacristy, and out into the sanctuary. His clandestine moves made him feel strangely exhilarated. He was not even sure what he was doing there or what this mission was about. He just needed to see the statue again and study it somehow. It was another piece of the puzzle that he felt certain would help him. David's emotions were racing through him to the point that he found his hands quivering as he made his way across the altar and toward the crèche. The church was quiet and lit only from the outside light coming through the stained glass windows.

It splashed the church interior with a rainbow of colored light and gave it an eerie essence of mystery. The multicolored light only buttressed his feelings of excitement and foreboding.

David literally leaped over the communion rail to make his way to the manger scene. He rounded the corner of the stable and focused his vision inside it.

The manger scene was as before, the baby Jesus on a bed of straw in the simple manger, arms extended outward in a heavenly gesture. The baby had a slightly turned-up mouth that projected a welcome to this place and his grace. Mary was leaning slightly toward the baby and wore an expression of wonder and joy. The shepherds were gathered around the manger and appeared transfixed on the baby. This was all as it should be, but David's attention was riveted on the Saint Joseph figure. At first he focused in on the clothing to reaffirm they were indeed the same as what he had seen in the bible illustration and in the visions of the man. The Saint Joseph statue was in the same position and wearing the same attire as before, but its lifeless, stone eyes, instead of admiring the new leader of the Christian world, were staring at David! This was more than a shock for David, and it caused him to stumble backward. He almost fell down, and he felt a sudden and strong nausea. He went to his knees but could not take his eyes away from the statue. The statue returned the stare.

David found his legs again and backed away from the manger as if it were a crouched tiger waiting to spring. He could not believe what he was seeing. This was not just some hallucination; the statue was physically altered from its previous orientation. This was a new sensation, and he was unnerved. He knew in his mind that this was impossible, but there it was right in front of him. His fear started to culminate in the pit of his stomach. It built into a storm inside of him. This church had always been a sanctuary of quiet and peaceful solitude, but suddenly it was scary and perplexingly alien. He could feel his breath shorten and sweat form on his face and hands. He had to escape the church and the staring statue.

He turned and broke into a run. He ran through the sacristy and toward the back door where he had entered only moments before. He burst through without bothering to relock it. There was a short set of steps leading from the back door to the sidewalk below and David was just about to take the five quick steps in one leap when he unexpectedly found himself face to face with Father Donovan at the bottom of the stairs. He grabbed the handrail to stop his momentum. They were both caught by surprise and stared at each other for a wordless second. Father Donovan's look told David of his surprise and disappointment at finding one of his altar servers in a compromising situation at the church.

"David, I have to say I'm most surprised to find you here at this time today. May I ask what it is you are doing exiting the church from this doorway? A doorway that, I might add, is normally locked."

"Father," David stuttered as he continued to face the priest, now with a look of embarrassment. "I was having some conflicts and wanted to spend some time in the church. Sorry that I used the key to enter at a bad hour. I did not intend any harm."

"I see," said the priest, a scowl planted on his face. He did not immediately buy into this flimsy story.

"I'm really sorry, Father. I really didn't mean any harm to anyone." David was not really sure if he was sounding convincing because he knew he was lying about his real reason for being there. He let the words hang in the air, hoping they would sway the priest.

"OK, David. I hope I don't find anything amiss inside. Aren't you serving at tonight's midnight mass?"

"Yes, Father, I'm scheduled for tonight's midnight mass. I will see you then, and Merry Christmas." David displayed an almost silly smile to help cement his hoped-for exit from both the church and this very uncomfortable conversation.

"Well, let's go inside the church and discuss what is troubling you. It seems like an opportune time, don't you think?"

David did not want to spend one more second speaking with the priest, much less go back to the scene he had just escaped. He stammered as he stared at his feet, hoping to find a response written somewhere on his shoe that would give him a clean getaway. His shoe only stared back at him as if to say, "you are on your own with this priest." David finally just nodded to Father Donovan. He backed away to let Father Donovan lead the way into the church, as he did not want to go first into this now hauntingly disagreeable building.

David followed the priest into the sacristy and then into the sanctuary. They rounded the altar, genuflected, and the priest led David to the first row of pews, where he sat and gave David a leveled look that said, "Sit here." David followed dutifully. From his vantage point, he could view the crèche, but he purposely kept his gaze away from that direction. He did not want to see the statue again.

"David, what has been troubling you to such an extent that you would make a clandestine entry into the church on Christmas Eve day? You must admit this is not expected behavior for a man your age."

David's mind was racing. He had no idea what he was going to tell the priest that would sound plausible and get him out of this menacing place as soon as possible. He was also struggling to keep his eyes from wandering to his left and viewing the manger. He did not want to have to fight off a new wave of emotions while also dealing with the inquisitive priest. He sat nervously in his seat waiting for the priest to take the lead, as he was not ready to volunteer yet another fabricated story to provide cover for the unbelievably bizarre events that were actually taking place.

"David, you are clearly distraught and seem almost, well, anguished. I have never known you to be so on edge. You know, it is cathartic to openly speak to an adult about things that trouble you. Life can seem much more complicated at your age than it will seem when you are older. I'm not diminishing your current anxiety or trying to belittle it. What do you think really brought you to the church this morning in such a state that you would enter without permission?" Father's voice was calm and soothing. David found himself wanting to tell the priest everything that was happening and force the priest to take on this burden with him.

David sat quietly and reflected on what he should do. He did not want to disclose this because the fewer people who knew, the less chance it had to get out into the small town gossip circles, the prospect of which made him shudder. As he pondered his dilemma, the environment of the church, presence of the priest, and his own Catholic indoctrination slowly presented him with a solution. He considered his idea for a few seconds in an attempt to find fault with it before springing it on the priest. The more he considered it, the more he felt his confidence build in pursuing this solution with Father Donovan. He turned to face the priest with a newfound look of confidence.

"Father, would you be willing to hear my confession?" David had suddenly realized that he could talk about it with the priest within the closeted and promised silence of the confessional. Catholic doctrine would not allow the priest to disclose anything heard in the confessional, and David knew that priests would not violate that trust.

"David, are you sure confession is the right venue for discussing what is troubling you? Is there some personal sin that has you upset?" Father Donovan lowered his bushy eyebrows as he studied David's face.

"Yes, Father, please, I need to have my confession heard. I know this is a bit unusual at this time when you have so much preparation in front of you for Christmas, but believe me, this is a very unique situation that I really need your input on."

"David, you are obviously experiencing something unusual, so I can hardly turn you and your request away. All right, let's go to the confessional then. I will meet you there. I need to get my surplice and purple stole." Father Donovan rose and made his way toward the vestment storage closet.

Once Father Donovan had donned his confessional garb, he led the way, keeping a wary eye on David as he trailed behind him.

A Catholic confessional is a small room about the size of a phone booth. One such booth is for the repenting soul and the adjacent booth is for the priest who sits facing outward. The confessional booth is dark and has a mesh screen between the priest and the confessor. The screen allows uninhibited verbal communication between priest and confessor, but they cannot see one another. The confessor kneels facing the priest, who sits at a right angle to the person confessing.

David began the practiced confessional prayer. "Bless me, Father, for I have sinned. My last confession was a month ago. These are my sins." David did not continue on with the normal litany of sins that traditionally follow this introduction. He had never engaged in a confession that wasn't a practiced "standard package" of sins. He had never really entrusted the inner parts of his soul to the priest, and he now almost regretted his decision to ask for this confession. He could hardly just list some simple sins after all the drama leading up to this moment with Father Donovan.

David let the silence settle between them. The darkness of the confessional seemed to be an ally to David as he contemplated his rash decision to take this to the secrecy of the confessional. Finally, without any other viable option, David took a deep breath and slowly related his story to Father Donovan. Once he began to speak, the events of the past few days flowed out of him as if he were speaking only to himself. The visual barrier between he and the priest provided a sanctuary that allowed his story to flow. With each word he felt weight lifted from his psyche or maybe his soul. As he spoke, the story became something familiar to him, something that was his alone. His voice carried without hesitation, and he soon forgot that the priest was there, only inches away. He did not really consider or care that the story was not really confessing sins but relating a tale that may well cause the priest to question his sanity.

Father Donovan did not interject anything into the boy's tale, and he let David continue unabated. This was without a doubt the strangest confession he had ever heard. He noted as well that it was difficult to identify any sin, but nonetheless, he was obliged to treat this within the confines of the confessional and the standards of the Catholic Church. He found himself sitting on the edge of his seat in rapt attention to every detail of this strange narrative. He was not sure whether to think this lad was completely losing his mind or that there might be some threads of truth to it. He knew David well enough to know he was not one to fabricate fantastic tales. David had matured early for his age. This entire repertoire did not fit with the boy he knew David to be. Father Donovan wanted to connect this to his faith, but he was uncomfortable jumping to such a conclusion without some tangible evidence that he himself could witness. It did give him pause, however, to think about the saints he had studied about all his life. Many of those were witnesses to visions of Jesus, Mary, or other heavenly beings. Was he now a witness to such an event? Could this naïve teenager actually be a conduit to such a heavenly connection? Regardless of the validity of David's story, the priest knew that for the boy's sake, he had to deal with it as if it was true. When David finished, the priest turned toward him with a start. Even though neither he nor David could see each other through the confessional screen, the priest found this last piece of information very troubling. The boy had either really seen something here in the church that shouldn't be, or he had completely imagined it. Father Donovan had to consider that either reality was deeply disturbing.

"David, I'm not sure what to say to such a . . . a . . . well, such an unusual confession. I don't think there is a real sin here, unless the visions tie to some other events in your life. Is there anything else to tell me?"

"I'm not sure what you are thinking of, Father. I don't know of anything else to add that might be relevant."

"Well, in that case, have you told this to anyone else?"

"No, Father, just you at this time." David knew this was not the truth, even though he had not told Becky of the most recent events. He felt it best to keep all of this contained within the confessional until he could determine what to do about it.

"David, it's hard to say what this is about for you. It could be something spiritual, of course, but we have to consider that it might be some other type of hallucination. Although I can see how upsetting these visions are to you when they happen, it does not seem that any harm is connected to these events, at least not so far. That being the case, I recommend that you pray the rosary to ask God for further guidance and to either send a clear message or to relieve you of these traumatic experiences. Why don't we both go up to the crèche and check to see if Saint Joseph is looking where he is supposed to and not out toward you?"

David agreed, and he and Father Donovan made their way from the confessional at the back of the church toward the crèche. David found that having lifted the story from his soul and sharing it with Father Donovan, he had renewed strength, and he was not so afraid to see the troublesome statue again. As they approached the manger scene, David could see from a distance that Saint Joseph's head was facing as it should be and was not pivoted toward him or the back of the church. He felt that he must be having some kind of hallucinations, but as soon as he considered this, he remembered Becky seeing the footprints in the snow yesterday.

"Father, I see that the statue is as it should be," David said plaintively.

"Yes, it appears so, David. Why don't you take some time to pray here in the sanctuary while I attend to preparations for Christmas Eve and midnight mass services? I'm sure that regardless of what is happening to you that some prayers will help soothe your soul."

"Ok, Father, I will take some time to do that."

"God bless, son. I hope things clear up for you about this. Let me know, OK?"

David nodded his agreement with the priest and then knelt in the front row to spend some time in silent prayer. Father Donovan gave him a squeeze on the shoulder and then made his way back to the sacristy.

Being Catholic, David was accustomed to rote prayers that were prepared and prepackaged by the church such as Our Father and Hail Mary. He realized he did not have as much practice in just letting his thoughts flow to God. He spent time thinking about all that had happened and the wisdom of telling Father Donovan. As time passed, he found himself speaking to God and asking for guidance and help to understand what was happening to him and why he was seeing Saint Joseph. He realized that with all this happening to him, he had not yet considered prayer to help provide him some answers or at least some relief. He decided he had been remiss in not asking for the help of Jesus and maybe even Saint Joseph himself in gaining some understanding of his situation. He decided he would spend more time in prayer on this; after all, he didn't have anything to lose at this point and it was a saint, or so it appeared, that was tormenting him.

After an indeterminable amount of time spent praying and asking Jesus for help, he got up to leave and gave the statue one last look to make sure it was still facing toward the baby Jesus. It was.

H e got into the truck and decided to drop in on Becky to confirm that she had really seen those tracks yesterday. He started the ice-cold truck and made his way slowly toward her house. As the truck nosed its way on the icy road, David contemplated whether to tell Becky about the bible pictures, the statue, and the confession. As a Protestant, Becky had dubious thoughts about confession in general, so he was not sure he wanted to travel down that road with her.

On the way to her house, he drove by the car lot where he had seen the 1955 Chevrolet Bel Air for sale. He told himself he needed a break from his stress, so he stopped along the road and made his way into the lot. As he approached the car, he noticed it had been washed and polished, which was a bit unusual in the winter months. David walked around the car looking at every detail and imagining cruising the streets of Seltice Falls in this beauty. He pressed his face to the glass on the driver's window to help facilitate the image of gripping the steering wheel as he drove along Main Street with Becky clinging to his arm.

"Hey, David, what do you think? Quite the ride, eh?" It was Forrest Mandle. Forrest was about two years older than David and had worked at the Chevy dealer since high school. Forrest did not have escape dreams about leaving

Seltice Falls and was happy to have employment here in his hometown. So here he was washing cars and doing light mechanical duty, for which he had an aptitude, and it suited him just fine.

"Yes, Forrest, I love this car. Has it been sold?" David was hoping that it was just getting cleaned and that it had not been sold, at least not yet!

"As a matter of fact, it has been sold. I've got to get it ready to deliver today! I think somebody is getting a nice car for Christmas, that's what I think." Forrest's response indicated his admiration for the sporty two-door with red-and-white two-tone colors.

"Sure is a nice car," was all David could muster, as his heart sank thinking that this car was not going to be on the lot any longer for him to dream about owning. "You are right. Someone is going to enjoy Christmas. Well, Forrest, have a great Christmas yourself."

"Sure, you, too, David. Maybe see you at midnight mass?"

"Yeah, as a matter of fact, I am serving tonight. See you there," David replied while still eyeing the four-wheeled dream maker. He was still relishing a vision of him and Becky seated side by side in the front of this shining beauty as they made their way down Main Street on a warm summer evening with all the windows rolled down to show off the hardtop design. David could not help but linger a bit longer to savor his thoughts of enjoyment in this world of his own.

Finally, with a weak wave to Forrest, he turned and trudged back to the homely but reliable farm truck. After starting the engine, he sat and contemplated everything, from the dreams of the Chevrolet Bel Air, to the strange experience with the Saint Joseph figure, to his confession with Father Donovan. He even smiled at himself a bit for being clever enough to share his story in the confessional and force the priest to be an unwitting participant in this extraordinary episode of his life. He felt certain that Father Donovan was quite perplexed as to what to think about all of it, which made him chuckle out loud to have put one on the priest for a change, not that it helped his situation in any way.

After sitting alone with his thoughts and waiting for the cold-blooded Ford's tepid heater to warm the cabin, he slowly shifted into gear and made his way toward Becky's house. He had not contacted her about dropping by, so he hoped that Mary Marston would not be upset. He was not too concerned about Becky, as he was confident she would welcome his visit.

He was more nervous than he expected as he pushed the doorbell button. After a moment, Roger Marston opened the door and eyed David up and down. Roger liked David but being the surrogate father, he felt it his duty to provide some sufficient intimidation to his little sister's boyfriend. Even though Roger was only a year older than David, there was an understood delta of maturity between them due to Roger's role as man of this household since his father's untimely death in the logging accident.

"What do you want?" Roger snarled through a grin.

"You know I came just to visit with you, Roger," David fired back with a slight turned-up smile, as he tried his best at humor to lighten the mood.

"David!" Becky squealed as she came up quickly behind Roger. "Roger, get out of the way and let David come in. It's freezing out there!"

Roger smiled at his sister as he yielded the doorway to her, but he made sure to give David one last stern grimace before he disappeared into the house.

Becky pulled David into the house and twirled her head around to see if her mom was watching before she gave him a warm embrace and a quick kiss. David was as stiff as the statues at church, as he knew he was in uncertain territory here in Becky's foyer. Fortunately, Becky did not linger but pulled him by the hand into the living room.

"What are you doing dropping by today? I'm glad you did. It's a pleasant, unexpected surprise."

"Well, you know it's Christmas Eve tonight and I thought it might be fun for us to do some last-minute shopping in town and enjoy the Christmas decorations in all the stores.

"David, that sounds fantastic! Let me ask Mom!" Before Becky could even look around for her mom, Mary Marston was already approaching.

"Well, David, this is an unexpected surprise. It's nice to see you again. What brings you out today?"

"Good afternoon, Mrs. Marston. It's very nice to see you today also. I was wondering if Becky might join me for some last-minute Christmas shopping and enjoying the decorations in town." David impressed himself with his quick thinking about why he was here. It sounded plausible enough.

"Well, David, that does sound like fun. I think that would be OK, but please be mindful that this is Christmas Eve and we have services tonight, as I'm sure you do as well. Becky needs to be home no later than 3:30 or 4:00 this afternoon. I hope I can trust that you will be able to respect this schedule?" Mary Marston's voice transmitted strength and maybe a mild warning via her tone. It was clear enough to David of her rigor regarding adherence to the required schedule.

"Mrs. Marston, you can be sure that we will be back on time. I completely understand your requirements and, of course, I have to be home as well. You know those cows don't know enough to take Christmas Eve off!" David's bit of humor did not seem to register in Mary

Marston's demeanor, but nonetheless she accepted David's commitment.

Becky was already tugging at David to go. She had quickly freshened up her makeup, ran a brush through her hair, and grabbed her purse. She kissed her mom on the cheek and hurried David out the door. She clung to his arm as they made their way to the truck, which thankfully was still warm. As they drove away they could see both Mary and Roger Marston watching them from the front room's large window.

"Becky, I'm sorry to have just shown up unannounced, but I really wanted to speak to you again about everything. Of course, we can do some shopping like I said, but before that can we just talk?" David spoke without looking at Becky. He did not really want to see her reaction yet.

"Of course, we can talk. You know me, I love to talk." Becky giggled at her self-effacing comment.

David parked the old truck in the back of one of the common parking areas near the center of town. With this being the last day before Christmas, there were not that many parking spots anyway so being in the back was not something that would look out of the ordinary or suspicious to anyone.

David related his experience at the library and the startling discovery he made in the bible illustrations and the seemingly impossible connection to Saint Joseph. Becky listened intently as he slowly related every detail that he could recall from the library. Becky resisted his conclusions at first as mere coincidences. But David reminded her of the footprints that she had witnessed just the day before and that this could not just be in his mind. Becky tried to deflect this stubborn piece of evidence, but in the end, she had to admit that she could not explain those clear depressions in the snow that were freshly made by no one she could see and tracks that came from and went nowhere. But to Becky this still did not rise to the level of connecting this experience with the bible illustrations and the specter.

Before Becky could really resolve this conflict in her mind to any satisfaction, David continued on with the day's events by telling her his experience with the statue at the church. This caused Becky to turn and look straight into David's eyes as if realizing that she was sitting here alone in this truck with a madman.

"The statue's head was turned toward you? Are you sure?" Becky said in amazement.

"Yes, exactly. I can't explain it any more than any of these other events, but there it was looking at me. Jeez, Becky, I don't know how any of this is happening. I'm just being honest with you about it. I can't really tell anyone else, you know." David turned to look at her as he finished this comment.

Although he told her about the encounter with the priest, he did not tell her about his confession. He didn't see any benefit in telling her, and he did not want to explain the concept of the confessional to his Protestant girlfriend. It seemed like too much work for the moment. David drew additional comfort in keeping Becky thinking she was his only confidant, at least at this point. There certainly was no danger that the priest would expose his story to anyone.

"So did the statue return to normal?" Becky asked.

"Yes, but not before my eyes or anything. It happened sometime before I left the church." David did not like to keep the unvarnished truth from Becky, and while this was not untrue, it was not in keeping completely with the facts.

"Well, let's suppose that somehow this is Saint Joseph that has been appearing to you," Becky started, as she wanted to analyze this entire sequence.

"What? Whoever heard of Saint Joseph appearing to anyone? Are you serious?" David said a bit incredulously.

"OK, for sake of argument anyway. Let's just say it is an apparition of Saint Joseph. OK?" Becky continued.

"Well, I don't see it, but OK. What are you thinking?"

"I was thinking that if it were such a vision, he would have both a reason for these visits and a reason why he chose you, and I guess, me, to some degree. Let's analyze it from that standpoint. The message would have to be one that you could interpret and do something about, right? Well, don't you think that makes sense?" Becky was probably the more analytical of the two. Even though David was very interested in science and discovery, this ethereal world experience was not so easy for him to catalogue.

"OK, I see your point. But I can't think why someone in Seltice Falls, Idaho, would merit such an experience or what I could possibly do to affect some kind of change in the world." David sounded puzzled. He had to admit that he had not really seriously considered this viewpoint.

"Well, maybe it's not to affect the outside world, maybe it's right here in Seltice Falls, or maybe just within yourself. You're the Catholic. Don't you guys have lots of saints that had visitations from Mary, Jesus, and maybe others?" Becky was pressing a bit now. She sensed she was forcing her farmer boyfriend to think in the large picture instead of just focusing on the experience itself.

"Yeah, I guess we Catholics have our visions and apparitions, but that was stuff that happened in the Middle Ages or something, not today. I don't know of any visions or appearances in the past century. I still don't see why this would be happening in Seltice Falls and to me. I mean, what is the purpose and why is the guy so mysterious? Why doesn't he just tell me what he wants or wants me to do? Why haunt me like some kind of poltergeist?"

"I don't know why he's doing what he's doing. I'm just asking you to think about why he's doing it. David, you're a science guy. Think about it, there must be a reason for his actions. He wouldn't just go through all these appearances without a purpose." Becky kept trying to focus David on a higher vision.

"That's assuming he is Saint Joseph or some such saint. What if it's just a ghostly spirit or something?"

"Well, I said let's assume for sake of argument that he is Saint Joseph or some saintly version of him. If we take that assumption then we have to conclude there is a purpose to all of this, wouldn't you agree?" Becky continued her argument.

"OK, if I take that position as you suggest, then what do you think he's trying to communicate to me? I don't know what he wants," David responded.

"I don't know, David. I haven't thought about it like that either, but I think we should consider this angle. Don't you think we should?"

Becky and David discussed what the possible motives might be that would explain all these events that David had experienced. They could not really come to a consensus on what could be driving the man. Their conversation ebbed and flowed, tracing one theme and then another. It was difficult to align each event to any specific item in David's life or behavior. Both Becky and David were good students, both attended church regularly, and they could not pinpoint anything in their young lives that was sinister or overtly evil. They discussed their minor offenses to what was right and good, but even this young couple understood that their transgressions did not rise to the threshold of sin that would merit a visit from a heavenly apparition. They discussed it until they both felt spent but did not conclude with any solid result.

Becky circled the conversation back to her starting point. "David, I still think we have to focus on why this guy . . ."

"Saint Joseph," David injected sarcastically.

"Whoever," Becky shot back. "Why this guy is visiting you. What is he expecting from you?"

"Visiting? Is that what you call it now? Visits are usually a lot more enjoyable than what I'm experiencing with this fellow," David responded.

Becky did not want to turn this into an argument, so she backed it down a bit. "OK, but just think about it and see if you can come up with anything that might fit into what I said. Can you do that?"

David begrudgingly agreed to consider it some more and see if he could conclude any connection between his small life here in Seltice Falls and a visit from heaven, no matter how ridiculous that sounded when he said it aloud.

They both laughed when he said it and this squeezed the tension out from inside the cab of the truck. For the moment they managed to vanquish their anxiety with laughter and, at the same time, concluded with a soft and passionate kiss. They held each other without any more words to clutter up the atmosphere.

They kissed lightly again and David broke the silence. "Let's do some last-minute Christmas shopping. We can just forget about the strange man or Saint Joseph or whoever he is that keeps bugging us. At least let's forget about him for a while and shop and enjoy Christmas Eve."

Becky agreed with another kiss, this one more passionate. "Let's go to the variety store. They always have a great mix of things, and I still need to get Roger something for Christmas. He's really hard to buy for, you know."

They strolled the snowy streets, window-shopping and holding hands, which helped both of them escape the mystery. They bought some stocking-stuffer gifts for family and some for their close friends, but they mostly enjoyed each other's company and companionship. Neither really understood it, but they both knew that this strange man had changed their relationship somehow; the experience had bonded them beyond what a normal young love would have achieved. They were sharing something that was beyond anything they or anyone they knew had experienced, and the fact that this was kept in a secret covenant between them bolstered this bond between them.

As they stopped for a hot chocolate at the drugstore fountain, David could not help but tell Becky about the beautiful Chevy at the local dealer that someone had purchased. "You should see it, Becky. It's a bright two-tone red and white with a beautiful interior. It hardly looks used and it's a two-door hardtop, which would really be a gas to cruise in the summer. I can see us riding down Main Street in it right now. I have to admit that I'm really envious of whoever is the lucky person buying it."

Becky was not interested in the car, but she was enchanted by David's flashing eyes as he excitedly talked about this dream car of his. She smiled softly and nodded as he continued to expound on the virtues of the Chevy. As David's dissertation slowed, she asked, "Did you ask who bought it?"

"I suppose I should have . . . but no, I didn't even think about it. I guess I was so disappointed that it was going to be gone and I was not going to be able to ogle over it anymore that subconsciously I didn't want to know who bought it. Stupid, I guess." David's voice trailed off.

"Oh, not necessarily stupid. Everybody wants things, David." Becky tried to soften his self-deprecation.

"I guess you're right, but this is Seltice Falls, not Seattle. There aren't that many nice cars to drool over here." David laughed as he fired this verbal missile at his hometown.

They continued to chat about the car and the quality of the hot chocolate, as well as visiting with the soda fountain attendant, who was also a student at the school. Becky asked David to come for Christmas dinner at her mom's house, but David said it was not possible as his mom and dad insisted on him being home on Christmas Day. He did agree to do his best to negotiate a break from home late in the day after Christmas dinner so he could stop by and visit Becky and her family.

Their conversation could not help but drift back to the man and what had been happening over the past few days. They kept their speech discreet so as not to attract unwanted attention, but unfortunately the very act of being discreet in a town the size of Seltice Falls tends to draw unwanted suspicion. They decided to head back to the truck as it was getting later in the afternoon and they both had some last-minute wrapping to do before tomorrow. David drove Becky home, where they parted with another warm hug and kiss and wished each other a blessed Christmas and promised to see each other the next day.

David's mother was irritated with him when he arrived home, as she had expected to see him around during the day to help with chores and last-minute preparations for Christmas Eve and Day. He gave her enough of a heartfelt apology to quiet her but knew that he had let his mom down, which was something he didn't like to do, nor did often.

Janet Edmonds could detect something was amiss with her son, as mothers can often do. David was almost always punctual, polite, and thoughtful of others. Recently he had been more withdrawn, irritable, and frankly, a bit mysterious. She wanted to question him about it but she did not have any real grounds for being suspicious, so she decided to let things go unsaid at least for now.

David went straight to his bedroom and plopped onto his bed with an empty gaze upward. He just stared at the ceiling while thinking about all that had happened this day and the previous several days. Maybe Becky was right, perhaps there was some kind of message included in the visions of the man, or Saint Joseph. Saint Joseph! A man that lived two thousand years ago was now popping up in Seltice Falls? The pit of his stomach lurched when he thought about the possibility of this really being a heavenly vision, and he felt frightened and alone with this perplexing mystery. He shuddered as he considered the scope of possibilities surrounding his experiences. He did not want to close his eyes, as he was fearful that his mind would use this as a catalyst to spin off into numerous theories to explain the visions of the strange and troublesome man. To combat his own mind, he stared at his ceiling. There he found a focal point. In the light of day, it was only a twist of texture on the ceiling but in this moment it represented a place where his mind could focus and escape, and find some solace. The longer he stared at it, the more comforting it became, like an ally to him, nonjudgmental and innocuous.

His mind weaved scenarios, everything from his sanity eroding to him having a spiritual visitation, to the possibility of some scientific explanation of light and sound conspiring to perplex him. No matter the route his mind traveled, he could not assemble enough meaningful facts to draw a useful hypothesis that would satisfy his scientific evaluation or the friendly texture design on the ceiling.

Were there some elements of a true message to be found from this man and his harassing visits? If this was somehow a real apparition from heaven, then what in the world would the actual Saint Joseph be doing visiting him? He was not a bad person but certainly not saintly either. Of all the places and people in the world, why would the heavens think that Seltice Falls and David Edmonds would merit such a visit? He could not fathom that this was really Saint Joseph trying to communicate with him, but he had to admit that he could not completely rule this out of the list of potential explanations. He wanted Becky to be here with him, lying in his room with him, not in a sexual context but to hug him and help him understand it. He had always relied on his parents in the past for such support and understanding, but now, somehow, the thought of Becky was more comforting to him. He felt sure that his parents would dismiss these experiences as products of an overly active imagination, which David knew he possessed. He continued to focus on the small spot of texture on the ceiling.

Suddenly, the texture spot had a face and something of a glow to it. The face was a familiar one, the face of the man. David's fixed focus on the texture spot was no longer voluntary; it was locked onto the face. The man's expression was softer than previously, not smiling but not scolding either. It was the face of a man with something to share, something to give. It had the same smile of the face but not so much of the mouth. Dave watched as the intensity of the illumination increased, and it seemed the physical size of the face grew. As the face continued to grow, the expression remained almost constant, except for an almost-imperceptible increase in the semi-smiling countenance of the expression. David felt himself becoming almost comfortable with the now-familiar man, even though he was still on the uninformed side of this relationship.

As the face continued to grow larger and David's stare continued to be focused on it, he suddenly realized that the face was not really growing larger but was actually descending from the ceiling, giving the appearance of growth. This unnerved David, and he wanted to move off the bed to escape it, but he could not move a muscle. He was frozen in place and the comfort of familiarity quickly evaporated like smoke from a dying campfire.

"David, are you ready?" the unexpected voice coming at David was startling but not enough to unshackle David from his frozen position on the bed. The voice was familiar but did not seem to fit the face, and David noticed that the man's mouth had not moved. "David, David, are you ready for your work?" again the voice was familiar but clearly did not fit the voice of a man that looked like this man. The face was now not as clear as before but was still growing and descending toward him. David could only remain frozen and try to adjust his vision to better focus and see the encroaching face more clearly.

The face continued to advance, and as it did so, it kept losing resolution. David had to squint and concentrate to try to bring it into better focus as it approached. Even though the advance of the face toward him was unnerving, he noticed that the expression had softened even more. Then he felt the soft squeeze of a hand on his shoulder, which caused a reflex move that made him jump from the bed. As his eyes jerked open, he found himself staring up into his mother's face.

"David, wake up. Are you OK?" Janet Edmonds's expression was one of concern. "You were having some kind of nightmare or something, the way you were thrashing on the bed. Is everything OK, David?"

David took in his mother's face and just as quickly snatched a look at the ceiling texture, which had just been the object of concern and host of the face. The texture had returned to its static state; the face was gone.

"Sorry, Mom. I guess I was having a bad dream. I didn't realize I had dozed off. When did you come into the room?"

"I came in just now to get you up to start chores. It's time to milk the cows. Are you all right?"

"Yes, I'm OK. I just had a bad dream. I'll get ready for chores. Sorry if I startled you."

Janet Edmonds backed slowly away from David's bed but held her eyes firmly on him. Although David did not notice the concern she had for her son, it clearly was etched across her face and imbedded in her furrowed brow. She slowly withdrew from the room but in a reverse fashion so she could continue to study her son.

David pushed the image of the face from his mind and quickly changed his clothes to start his milking routine. As he readied himself for the barn, he pondered the more serene, almost happy look on the face at this last encounter. Maybe it was just part of his dream and was not even related to other actual visitations. He hoped it was a softening of the man's demeanor.

Christmas Eve was usually a joyous and happy time in the milking pit, as the anticipation of the festivities of the evening and the following day captured everyone's imaginations and thoughts. But tonight was different for David. He went through the mechanical motions of milking the cows with efficiency but clearly without the joy that this evening usually brought. Paul Edmonds finished his feeding work and joined David to help finish the milking. Paul noticed the lack of enthusiasm in his son for this special day, and although he did not mention it to David, he studied his son for a clue of what might be the root of his distraction tonight. Paul was also aware of how David's behavior had been out of character the past few days but did not want to inflame it by quizzing him, so he held his tongue and together they worked in silence with the sounds of the milk parlor keeping them company.

David and his dad finished up the chores for the evening and headed into the house for a festive Christmas Eve dinner.

The Edmonds family said some additional meal prayers related to the Christmas celebration and then enjoyed a dinner fit for such an occasion. Janet Edmonds put out a spread of prime rib beef roast, potatoes, broccoli, beans, homemade rolls, and all the condiments to accompany such a feast. David managed to find his appetite, not difficult for a teenage boy, and ate heartily, which gave his mom some relief from her concern. In truth, the meal, conversation, and the gaiety of the evening helped to break David from his worries. As the meal progressed, he soon found himself feeling lighthearted and anticipating the Christmas celebration ahead.

The family had a tradition of a prayer vigil before the crèche in their living room as part of their annual Christmas Eve celebration. Janet Edmonds always made sure that her family stayed focused on the birth of Christ and not so much on the jolly elf in the red suit. Although the children probably would have been fine with skipping this part of the evening, they also found comfort in the solemnity of the prayers and, of course, making their mom happy.

The evening was swept away in swirls of laughter, memories, and carols, as well as everyone speaking about what Christmas morning might bring. Katy, Judy, and Michael were bundles of barely restrained energy as they carefully studied the colorful and brightly wrapped packages nestled happily under the tree. They also felt special to be able to join their parents and older siblings at midnight mass, which was well past their bedtime. Janet and Paul liked taking them because they would be exhausted when they got home, which prevented too early of a rising the next day when the assault on the presents started. David was thinking about that 1955 Chevy he had seen today at the lot and wondered if he would have a chance of getting his own "set of wheels" this Christmas. He felt that the joy of getting a vehicle would help him erase the memories of the man and his bothersome visitations. As he watched the twinkle of the lights on the tree, his mind parlayed that into the shine from the chrome of his own car. Now that would be exciting!

Soon it was time to get ready for midnight mass. The family dressed in their best finery for the occasion. David normally wore a jacket and tie but because he would be one of the mass servers, he would be wearing the black cassock and white surplice, and so he only dressed in slacks and a button-down shirt, approved by his mother, of course.

The family piled into the waiting and cold Buick for the trip to church, a trip shared by a lot of other Catholics. A light snow began falling as David made his way to the sacristy to dress for the mass. The Christmas midnight mass was celebrated as a High Mass, which was a mass of additional ceremonies, and the liturgy was sung as opposed to just spoken. At this High Mass, there were four servers assigned, two primaries who performed the bulk of the attendant functions and two secondary servers who mostly filled out the ceremonial positions required by the church.

David was glad that he and Ronnie Hovett were the primary servers tonight and they would not have to fill the secondary positions. The secondary positions were always left to the more junior members of the server roster. In this case, Russell Kraft and Ricky Stranger were the lucky junior servers tonight. They were both two years younger than David and Ronnie, so they were subservient to them.

David avoided the crèche as they prepared the sanctuary for the service. He did not want to even look at the Saint Joseph statue for fear of what he might see there. He made sure that the preparations he took on were away from the manger scene. The other boys wanted to work around the crèche so this did not raise undue suspicion from them. The church congregation was large, which was normal for Christmas midnight mass, as many Catholics attended this service only and did not bother to return until the following year, with maybe the exception of attending on Easter Sunday.

The mass progressed according to schedule, which suited David just fine. The bible readings were the traditional book of Luke, which struck David with unexpected clarity as he had just spent time in the library studying these very verses. As he listened again to the story of the first Christmas according to Luke, he started to become anxious and beads of sweat began forming on his back and forehead. He could not help but try to peek at the manger scene to study the Saint Joseph figure. As before, the crèche was positioned away from the altar where David was serving mass, so he could not see the figure from where he was kneeling. He wasn't sure he wanted to see it, but he knew that he would have to face it sooner or later as part of the mass.

After the sermon, which David had trouble staying focused on because of the anxiety building within him, it was time to once again light some incense and do the blessing of the statues. David and Ronnie were in charge of getting the incense burner loaded and the burner started. They performed their duties flawlessly, although for David it was probably more perfunctory than anything else. Once Father Donovan had put the incense onto the burner and the familiar scent of it filled first the sanctuary and then the rest of the church, the servers and Father Donovan did the traditional blessing of the congregation by walking the perimeter of the church and swinging the incense burner in such a way as to send its slightly sweet, slightly acrid smell toward the parishioners and throughout the church.

The culmination of the march around the church concluded in front of the crèche. David found that now that he was in front of the Saint Joseph statue, he could not raise his eyes to look at it. The fear had built inside of him as he approached the manger scene. He found himself looking at the foot of the stable. The cheap cloth curtain that skirted the stable was surprisingly ugly. Although he had seen it numerous times before, he had never really considered its aesthetics. His eyes followed the bottom of the skirt in a vain attempt to keep from looking at Saint Joseph.

Although Father Donovan had knowledge of David's strange visions due to the confession, he did not seem to notice David's behavior in front of the crèche, as he was focused on the ceremony at hand and had a larger than normal audience. Father Donovan recited the required prayers before the manger scene while dosing it with a generous cover of incense smoke. David was happy for the smoke as it camouflaged his distracted demeanor from the priest and his follow servers.

David finally could not resist any longer and slowly raised his gaze to encounter the Saint Joseph figure. He was certain that in front of the congregation, the figure would be as expected, facing the Christ child in the manger and as stoic as such a statue should be in this scene. To David this clearly was a reasonable expectation. How could it be otherwise?

This, however, was not to be, not tonight. To his horror, as he raised his eyes to engage the statue, David's tentative and frightened gaze was met straightaway with Saint Joseph's. He was looking straight at him; there was no mistaking it. Worse than this, the statue's eyes were life-like, not as one would encounter with a porcelain figure. David knew what a statue's eyes should look like, and this was *not* it. These eyes were watery, with the depth and quality of human eyes. David did not know how to interrupt this extremely unnerving encounter. His knees started to weaken and he felt as if he might urinate from the sheer overwhelming anxiety. He forced himself to look away from the statue. He looked to his fellow celebrants and could see they had no reaction to what had just happened. They were going through the ceremonial rituals, oblivious to this statue's strange countenance. He quickly pivoted his head back to the statue and once again, to almost no surprise, he found that Saint Joseph was obediently facing the Christ child just as he should be. He could not help but think that he must be losing his mind, but as soon as he thought this, he remembered once again that Becky had also experienced part of his encounter. Could she have just been humoring him so that he would not feel so troubled? It was the first time he considered this possibility. Becky's reaction certainly had not seemed contrived. He could not resolve this in his mind.

The party of celebrants finished the ceremonies and worked their way back to the altar, while David rotated his head one last time to peek at Saint Joseph, but he found nothing out of place now, with Saint Joseph or anyone else.

For the rest of the service, David felt removed from reality, as his mind jumped around between all of the experiences of the past days. He wanted to find some kind of final resolution to all of the events, but none was to be found in the jumble of his thoughts. He was so absorbed in his thoughts that he didn't even notice his family as they filed up for communion. His mom noticed his distant demeanor and could not help but extend a mother's worry toward her son. Janet Edmonds kept watching David as much as she could while he finished serving the mass.

David was stoic on the ride home and kept his view out the window. He didn't notice his mother's concerning looks.

It was past midnight when they arrived home. The Christmas Eve air was cold and crisp and the late hour had subdued everyone's enthusiasm for the holiday. The family filed out of the Buick and made their way into the warmth of the farmhouse. Paul Edmonds had not really noticed anything too out of the ordinary with David, but Janet's motherly instincts continued to shadow him with her eyes as David made his way into the house. David moved without the energy a watchful parent would anticipate for Christmas.

"OK, gang, let's all get into our pajamas and make our way off to bed," Paul Edmonds put forth in an attempted jolly voice but was clearly more stern than jolly.

Everyone was compliant enough, as even the young ones were tired and ready for bed. David gave a stiff kiss to his mom and a nod to his dad as he made his way to his bedroom. He sat on the bed for some time and stared blankly at the wall ahead. His mind was not racing but rather floating, trying to capture some essence from all the events at the church tonight and in the previous days. He eventually climbed into bed and stared at the ceiling instead of the wall. The stress of the past week had worn him down and he fell asleep quickly.

The fog was floating effortlessly across the street and dipped between the buildings like water cascading over stones. The density of the fog was intermittent as it moved and undulated over the ground. David looked down the street; it was familiar but also had a foreign quality to it. The form of the buildings looked correct, but they did not have the expected detail and resolution, as if the fog had penetrated the exteriors and sculpted their features to fit its mood. He found himself walking down the middle of the street, his pace deliberate and steady but slow. He was not sure where he was going or why he was there. He recognized the form and placement of the buildings and realized he was on Main Street. His gaze remained straight ahead as if looking for something. His footfalls were soft on the pavement and left barely an audible trace in the fog-shrouded air. He continued to walk steadfastly down the street toward something. What, he did not know.

A short distance ahead of him, slightly visible through the fog, stood the man. David was not surprised to see him; in this venue it was almost expected. The fog wafted in and out around the man, and David's view of him was intermittent at best. Still, there was no doubt that this was his now-familiar nemesis. David continued his steady pace down the middle of Main Street, his focus now fixed on the man. The man was not looking toward David but instead in the opposite direction. His heart began to race as he closed the distance between them.

Before he knew it, he was within a few feet of the man. He was expecting him to disappear or vanish as he had in the past, but the man remained steady on the foggy corner. David kept walking without approaching the man and, in fact, walked past him without really looking directly at him. As he walked past he wanted to look at the man, shout at him, something, but he found his head was fixed in a forward-looking position, and he could not seem to turn it from side to side.

As David continued walking, he could sense the man's presence or gaze on his back. His pulse continued to quicken, and he felt sweat forming on his back. Suddenly, he heard the man's footsteps approaching him from behind, directly behind. His stomach lurched with a pang of fear. He wanted to twirl around and confront him, but somehow knew that he would not challenge him in this manner. His body would have none of it and continued the forward march.

The man's pace was swift, and David soon found himself walking side by side with this fellow. Without explanation, David now found his muscle control enough to pivot his head and look at this strange figure; sure enough this was the same person he had seen on multiple occasions. The man did not return David's gaze but continued to look straight down the street as he walked step for step with David. This was the first time he was in close proximity with David. The beard, long hair, the colorful tunic, and the sandals were all as he had seen before. David studied the man as they walked in step down the middle of the street.

"Who are you?" David finally blurted out.

"David, you know who I am," the man responded.

David almost jumped back as he was not expecting the man to speak, much less to address him by name. David and the man continued their strange march as David studied him ever closer. He considered his theories about who this man looked like and the connections to the crèche statue and the bible pictures.

"You look like Saint Joseph. Is that who you are?" David found his nerve and queried further.

"You know who I am," the man repeated.

"How would I know who you are? You appear in different places and then disappear without ever speaking to me. I have no idea who you are or what it is you want with me," David retorted with an almost angry voice.

A silence formed between them as they continued to walk, both with their vision focused ahead. David tried to rest his mind for a short moment.

"Where are we going?" David let the identity question drop and moved on to more practical issues.

The man did not provide a verbal response; instead he increased his pace to put himself slightly ahead of David.

"Am I to follow you now?" David asked.

David kept pace while studying the man more closely. For the first time the man was right there with him and was not vanishing or doing some other parlor trick. There was no doubt in David's mind that this was indeed the same man he had faced previously. David also noticed that the man was carrying the same walking staff he had seen him carry before. He studied the staff and thought about its familiar look. As his eyes navigated from the staff to the man and back, he realized that the staff was the same one held by the Saint Joseph statue in the crèche at the church. This caused the hairs on the back of his neck to stand up, and he shuddered.

"Are you some kind of magician or con man or something?" David blurted out as he stared at the man's face.

Without breaking his forward gaze, the man sternly responded, "You know who I am, David."

This time David was compelled to respond, "Why do you say that? I have no idea who you are or why you are bothering me."

"You may not know why I am, as you say, bothering you, but you know who I am," the man responded with an impish grin that belied a similar expression from his forward-facing eyes.

"I can assure you that I don't know who you are. I know who you appear to be but that can only be an appearance." David was finding his resolve to fend off this man's position.

The man almost laughed in response. "You know very well who I am. You just do not want to accept it."

"Accept what?" David shot back, now getting a bit irritated.

"Do you not accept your own faith that you profess every day? Do you deny the very faith that you proclaim on this very special holiday? Do you deny him?" The man's tone became more stern and adult like.

"Deny him? Who? I thought we were speaking about you and why you are appearing to me and no one else. I don't deny anything. I would like a straight answer," David stated strongly.

The man actually laughed aloud but did not break his stride or look away from whatever it was they were walking toward. "He is denied constantly, every day, and more by those who proclaim to worship him than by anyone who despises him. It is not a denial of words but a denial of action. What is a man's being but that which is truly only shown by his action? A man's words are meaningless; denial is never so simple. You deny me now because your faith is

139

not as strong as your words would have others believe. As you can see, David, it is not so simple to be confronted with having to act on one's faith. The person who acts on it has true faith; the person who can only speak it is an impostor, not to the true one, but to himself."

David did not have a response that he wanted to put forth. He felt that there might be too much truth in what the man was saying and his response would only indict him, so he walked in silence and pondered the man's convicting words.

Except for the rap of their soles on the pavement, they continued down the street in silence. David thought of all the experiences of the past few days. If this apparition was really Saint Joseph, then why was he appearing to David in some lonely little town in Northern Idaho? As he considered that this might indeed be some kind of visitation from the saintly earthly father of Jesus Christ, his mouth started to go dry and he found he kept studying the man's features, his clothes, and his gait.

They were now approaching a house. It was a very modest house that clearly had seen better years. The house was tall and narrow with a small porch over the front door that seemed to cling to the house as if the house would rather toss it away. The old cedar siding had not seen the business end of a paintbrush in many years, and the paint that remained was slowly making a getaway in bubbles and peels. The yard was covered in snow and the fence that surrounded it had fallen down in most places. There were mysterious mounds in the snow that appeared to be tossed aside car parts or old lawn mowers that had long since expired from their former duties. The walkway had not been shoveled but rather trammeled down from use after the several snowfalls of the past few weeks.

"What are we doing here?" The state of the house made David uncomfortable. He was accustomed to his parent's well-kept farmhouse with a trimmed yard and shoveled walks.

"We are here for a visit. Since you know them we should visit on Christmas Eve." Again the man continued his march toward the house and into the yard.

David hesitated at the entrance to the yard. "I think you've made a mistake. I don't know anyone here!"

The man laughed again as he waited at the yard entrance for David to catch up. "Oh, but you do. Don't worry they will be glad to see you."

"You must be kidding! We can't go inviting ourselves into people's homes on Christmas Eve! I don't know who lives here and I certainly don't want to barge in on them tonight!" David protested.

"You need to trust me, my son. You do know them, you will see." The man remained calm as he spoke.

The man stepped forward and knocked softly on the door as David stood back in disbelief and fearful anticipation of what would happen next. There was a small window in the door, but David did not want to look through for fear of what he would see, especially in the company of this bothersome man.

The door suddenly opened with a small squeak. Although the doorway was not well lit, David saw a small, frail woman. She was middle-aged but carried more years on her face than could be discerned from the rest of her body and frame. She looked first at the man and then at David. It was a vacant look, not one of surprise or irritation that David would have expected from someone greeting unexpected strangers on Christmas Eve.

"Come in," she said flatly while shifting her gaze downward.

141

She stepped back as they walked into the small front room. The lighting was sparse and stingy. David followed the man into the room and past the woman. Although Seltice Falls was a small town, David was not familiar with this woman or this house. The man paused near the middle of the room where there was a small Christmas tree with some popcorn strings, homemade dough ornaments, colored-paper chains, and a few well-worn glass ball ornaments. David stood awkwardly beside the man and studied the room further. There were only a few very small gifts under the humble tree and no other decorations. In one corner stood a small wood-burning stove of sorts that appeared well worn and possibly not even very safe to use. But still it was dutifully working to keep the cold winter night at bay. He could see into the darkened kitchen and saw that it, too, was well worn and small, especially compared to the kitchen in his own house. As David and his unlikely companion continued to stand in the middle of the room, the woman sat down on an old, brown sofa that had seen better years. David could only watch as this bizarre scene unfolded, and he continued to stand awkwardly next to the man. Here they were in a stranger's home, one of them a man in strange robes, and this person had just let them in as if she knew them.

Into the room walked Johnny Bates, one of his classmates and a fellow server at church. Without saying anything or even looking at David or his companion, he sat on the tired old sofa next to the woman, who David instantly realized was Johnny's mother. He felt embarrassed to be in Johnny's home and to see how this family lived. He looked around the room with new perspective; this was Johnny's home. He did not know Johnny well, only from school and church, but here he was in his living room. Johnny was not a very popular boy. He kept to himself mostly and had

142

few friends. David had always thought that Johnny was a bit odd or maybe just not very friendly. He had never really thought about why Johnny didn't have many friends, and he now started to feel shame for not ever trying to make friends with him or to get to know him well enough to realize where he lived, especially in a town the size of Seltice Falls.

He looked around at the modest surroundings and the meager Christmas decorations and ornaments. He realized the stark contrast with his own home, with its better-quality furnishings and abundance of holiday decorations and gifts. His mind jumped to the memory of his family's gift-buying adventures in Spokane and the joy of his family's holiday celebrations.

As his eyes completed their sweep of the room, his gaze once again focused on Johnny and his mother sitting on the old sofa. He looked at Johnny, whose eyes were downcast, and realized that Johnny's life was much different than his own. He wondered if Johnny was excited for the future as David was, or if he could even envision it. It seemed to David that his mind was suddenly thrown open and an oncoming tide rushed in to expand his awareness. He felt a weakness in his knees and in his whole physical being that frightened him.

Mrs. Bates kept her empty stare straight ahead as if she were alone in the room. She was not old but she was aged beyond her apparent years on the planet, and her face looked like it hadn't known much laughter or many smiles.

"Is it going to be a joyous and happy Christmas?" The man's sudden voice exploding into the room caused David to jump. He turned to see who the man was speaking to. The man's focus was clearly on Mrs. Bates, and David quickly turned to see her response. David whirled his attention back to Mrs. Bates to see her reaction to this sudden and unusual outburst from the man. He was not sure that Johnny was even aware of their presence, even as they stood in the middle of the front room.

"It will be just another day," the woman paused, "well, at least I don't have to work. You know how things are here for Johnny and me. Life is hard, and we ain't very well liked in this town. Christmas? Yeah, we will make the best of it, but it will be pretty meager." The woman paused again. She had been speaking without lifting her eyes, but now she raised her head and looked at the man. "But you already know all that," she said to him. Then she looked straight at David and asked, "Why is he here anyway?"

"He is with me tonight. He is learning about life and his spirituality." As the man responded, David was chilled by the look the woman gave him. He felt almost criminal under her gaze.

She continued to peer straight at David. "Oh, it ain't your fault. You're just a kid that grew up lucky. Course, you don't know that, at least not yet. I do wish some of the kids would be nicer to my Johnny. He ain't always been dealt the best of hands, you know." She paused again before changing her stare back to the empty room. "I don't suppose you even really know Johnny, though, do you?"

David could only look upon her with embarrassment and fear, fear of what this visit was really about and why he was here. Johnny remained stoically silent and his eyes, and demeanor, remained downcast and empty. David had almost forgotten about his strange companion, who was still standing dutifully next to him in the sparse room.

David and the man continued to stand in the middle of the room with their gazes fixed on the sofa, where two lonely, sad people sat in silence. David realized that the Johnny he knew from school and church was not the Johnny sitting in front of him, at least not the Johnny he would have

144

described to others prior to this strange visit. He would have described Johnny as quiet and odd, and probably would say the guy was not very friendly. He never considered why this might be the case and never felt any need to think more deeply about it. Visions of his interactions with Johnny over the past few years were weaving their way in random bursts through his mind. Most of them made him feel more ashamed of himself.

One particular memory was of a seventh grade pickup basketball game on the playground at school. There was an uneven number of boys to choose from, and David was one of the captains that got to pick his team. In the end, Johnny was the last boy unpicked as both captains had hesitated in picking him, waiting for the other to make a move. David had known at the time that he should be kind and pick Johnny, but he was afraid that Johnny's poor athletic skills would handicap his team, so he stalled until the other captain had no choice but to pick him. David could still recall the look on Johnny's face at being the last pick and being someone that nobody wanted. This entire thought sequence fired through David's neurons in mere milliseconds but was impactful nonetheless.

Now David wanted to reach out to Johnny. It was a strange urge to go over and hug him and let him know that he was sorry for not being friendlier to him in the past, or at least kinder. It was strange how a glimpse into someone's personal life could create such a change in perception. David almost forgot where he was or who was standing next to him.

"It's time to leave," the man said flatly and turned to the front door to make his exit.

"What? I'm not even sure why we are here." David watched the man move toward the door but did not follow him.

"Yes, you do. You know exactly why we are here."

"No, I really don't know what we are doing here, and now you want to leave?" David objected.

"Yes, we are leaving. We are not finished." The man was now holding the front door open to the cold of the night and gesturing to David to make his exit.

"Finished? Finished with what?" David looked from the man back to the sofa where Johnny and his mother sat stoically as if they were the only two in the room.

"You know what," the man said flatly again as he made a stern gesture for David to exit.

"No, I don't know. I don't know why we are here, I don't know anything about being finished, and I don't even know who you are either!" David started his move toward the exit as he continued his protests.

"You may not have come to a realization about why we are here or what we are doing, but you do know who I am." The man's voice took on the irritated tone of an adult dealing with a child.

"I know who you appear to be, but I don't have any real proof of you being anything more than my imagination." David's voice took on the bearing of an adult argument, someone not quickly taken in by appearances.

"You know imagination and its temporal manifestations, and you know that this is not imagination. Don't con yourself, David." Now the man was being the mentor adult.

David knew what the man said was correct, that imaginations, even vivid dreams, were not anything like what he was involved with here. He thought about this actually being Saint Joseph, but his mind was resistant to such a reality, and his intellectual side said to keep his skepticism at the forefront of his observations and conclusions.

They exited the house and walked back out to the street. The night was still shrouded in fog, but it almost seemed

146

warm, like a summer evening, albeit an atypical summer evening as there were no sounds such as crickets singing or toads croaking. They walked in silence down the street, the man leading the way with David keeping pace at his side. Once again they found themselves in the middle of the deserted street, but clearly moving with authority toward some new objective.

They turned down another street and made their way to the Presbyterian Church. David hesitated, as it was unusual for Catholics to enter a protestant church. The man stopped and looked back at him with a scowl and sternly remarked, "Come down from your Catholic arrogance and follow me."

David responded by following the man into the sacristy of the church. As they entered, it was filled with daylight from the stained glass windows, and David had to squint from the unexpected brightness of the church interior. As they slowly walked forward, David was shocked to see that the church was filled with people, in the pews and even standing in the aisles. He stopped suddenly at this development and looked toward the man. The man gave a head gesture to continue walking with him. David was too stunned to resist and continued to follow. They made their way up the side aisle, in some cases pushing past other attendees who were standing because there was no more room in the pews.

Amazingly, no one paid any attention to them making their way toward the front of the church. They walked single file now, the man leading with David in apprehensive but obedient tow. David did not want to look around and see any people he knew, but he could not resist looking at the crush of people in the church. He wondered if they were all there for Christmas service and why they would be there in the middle of the night on Christmas Eve. Then he remembered the brightness of daylight streaming in through the windows. He wondered if it was suddenly morning and he had not noticed it as they walked down the street. His mind was really spinning as he tried to analyze his current venue. Clearly this was much more bizarre than his visit to the Bates' home.

As they made their way toward the front, he realized he had been in this church before, with Becky. This was the church she attended. It looked somewhat different than he remembered it, but he knew it was the same building. To his Catholic sensibilities the church seemed stark and plain, without the crucifix, statues, paintings, and ornamentation that he was familiar with in his own church.

His eyes were drawn toward the middle of the front aisle, where he saw a flag-draped casket surrounded by what seemed to be mountains of flowers and cards. David and the man continued moving toward the front of the church. With the sight of the casket, he also recognized the somber mood and the many wet eyes in the congregation. He knew that this person now lying in state was someone revered in life, at least in this community. He was so absorbed in taking in the scene that he almost forgot how strange the two of them must look to this congregation, walking silently to the front of the church during this somber ceremony They stopped at the front pew, where the immediate family of the deceased sat.

The man gestured David to enter the pew, which was not completely full as other congregants did not enter out of respect for the family. David gave the man a quiz-zical look that indicated his discomfort with entering this reserved pew on such an occasion. The man only gestured more firmly. David shook his head in quiet obedience and annoyed discomfort.

Cautiously, David looked down the pew at the aggrieved family. His nerves were jumping with anxiety at the prospect of what this family would think of these two odd fellows joining them at such a time.

David looked at the woman on the far end of the pew. Her face was covered in a dark veil and she kept a white handkerchief tightly gripped in her hand. She was a young woman, probably a little younger than his mother. As he continued to look, he realized that this was a familiar face, a face that he was sure he had seen many times before. He looked again at the casket and it struck him that the deceased was probably someone he knew, of course! Why else would this Saint Joseph fellow, or whoever he was, bring him here. As he studied the woman's silhouette, he noticed two children, a boy and a girl, sitting next to her. He did not have to study the boy to recognize him and his heart nearly burst from his chest. It was Becky's brother, Roger Marston! Although the girl next to him also had a veiled face, he knew instantly that this was Becky!

He started to shake with fear at what he was witnessing. He could not take his eyes from Roger and Becky, and although they were sitting mere inches from him, they did not pay any notice to him in the pew. As he looked at them, especially Roger, whose face was not covered, he noticed there was something odd about his appearance. He was smaller than he should be and looked younger. Becky was also smaller and looked almost childlike, not like the young woman he knew.

Roger's face was swollen with grief, and David could tell that he had spent a great deal of time crying. He now become aware that Becky was crying constantly through silent sobs, keeping her swollen, darkened eyes discreetly hidden behind the veil.

David studied the church, the casket, and then Becky, who so far had completely ignored him. He looked at the casket again and then back at Mrs. Marston and her two children. He looked back and forth as his mind fully realized that *they* were the immediate family! That could only mean that somehow he was in attendance of Mr. Marston's funeral from several years ago. He did not even try to think how this was possible. But he could not deny what his senses were showing him. The emotional empathy that enveloped him would not even give him the latitude to consider the oddity of sitting in this front pew with this grieving family. He could only look upon Becky and ponder the level of pain that she was obviously dealing with here today. He knew her as a bouncing, happy teen who seemed to have a zest for life and for making others happy. He had never witnessed her in anything remotely like this situation.

He remembered the accident that had taken her dad, but he did not know her then. He mostly remembered everyone, primarily his parents, speaking about it. He did not think that his parents attended the funeral as they were not close friends of the Marston family, but he didn't really recall. He was not about to look around for them, as he did not want to encounter them too. This was too much to absorb already.

"Such pain for a young person to absorb and try to make some sense of such a tragedy," the man, who was now seated next to David, whispered.

David turned and looked at him but could only nod his agreement before returning his eyes back to his Becky. He knew, of course, that her dad had been killed in a logging accident, heck, the entire town knew that, but he had never really considered what it must have been like for her to accept such grief and pain. How had she coped? She seemed such a positive, happy person. Was there a hidden part of her where she kept this dark part of her life locked away? He studied her face to see if he could better understand this girl he thought he knew. He wanted to reach out and touch her to try to comfort her aching heart. Even through the veil he could see that her face was red and swollen from hours of profound crying. He looked at her small hands that were rapidly churning a tear-soaked handkerchief into a wrinkled ball. He knew these hands but it was clear they were smaller and younger than the hands he was used to seeing on his girlfriend. He did not feel the boyish affectionate love that he normally felt for this girl; his feelings were now more empathetic, as he could see she was in relentless pain.

Without thinking about it, he reached over and put his right hand over her handkerchief-clutching hands. At first he only touched her lightly as he was not even sure she was aware of his presence, or if anyone was for that matter. His hand instinctively pressed down on her hands with an affection borne of his knowledge of her soul and her silent interior. She turned her head to look at him. There was a level of recognition in her eyes but her face remained stoic and without any change in expression. She studied David's face for what seemed like minutes but was really only seconds. It was not a look of study but rather a mostly blank stare. Becky did not smile, frown, or even acknowledge David, and after the long seconds had passed, she slowly turned her head back to the view of the casket. She did allow David's hand to remain upon her hands, even though there was no real acknowledgment of it.

David could only continue to study this face of immense sadness. He had never experienced anything like this in his life and could only imagine what it was like for Becky. He again felt a level of shame and guilt toward her. He had never really given too much consideration to this experience in her young life. The pain of the event was invading his psyche and his feelings for Becky now became a hybrid mix of intertwined affection, love, and empathy, an empathy like he had never known. He felt consumed by these over-whelming feelings.

"It's time to go." The man's whisper caught David off guard and startled him enough to make him jump.

"Go? Go where?" David whispered back without taking his eyes off Becky.

"It's time to go," the man repeated as he softly pulled at David's arm.

"We can't leave in the middle of the service!" David protested.

"We are not even supposed to be here and you know it." The man was being firm now, even though he still kept his voice in a whisper.

"Well, we are here and I don't want to leave Becky right now," David protested further.

"We are leaving now." There was no compromise in the man's voice, and David knew he had to follow his direction.

They both slowly rose and reversed their direction down the side aisle to make their exit. David thought this all very strange as the people standing in the aisle moved aside for them to pass but did not seem to react to them leaving in the middle of the service. David considered that this probably made sense as they hadn't reacted to them being there in the first place.

They exited the church and found that it was still dark outside; the shafts of light that had just been coloring the interior of the church were gone, and they were once again alone walking down the darkened winter street.

David's mind was completely absorbed in what they had just witnessed, so he just walked silently at the man's side. For his part, the man walked with a purposeful stride without looking at David or speaking.

They soon found themselves entering a neatly arranged neighborhood. It reminded David of Becky's street, but it wasn't. Once again the houses seemed slightly out of focus. They continued walking until the man stopped and looked toward a house on their left. This house was in sharp focus, unlike its contemporaries on either side of the street. David studied it. Unlike the Bates' house, this house was neat and trim with a well-maintained front porch, a fairly new paint job, and shoveled walks. It was a single-story bungalow with a large roofed front porch. There were soft lights burning inside, but David could not tell if anyone was home.

The man turned and started up the walk toward the front door. David did not even bother questioning him; he knew he would have to be a participant in whatever awaited them on the other side of the door.

They climbed the front steps and the man knocked on the door. David noticed a swing to one side of the cozy-looking porch. Normally, he would think this was ridiculous to be knocking on some stranger's door late at night on Christmas Eve but after the night's experiences thus far, he was dutifully following his companion's lead. He stood slightly behind and to the right of the man as they waited for someone to answer. David looked through the front room window and could make out a decorated tree and a sofa but not much else, as the light was limited.

The door suddenly opened. Standing there was Mr. Monroe, the hardware store owner. Mr. Monroe was wearing workpants and an old flannel shirt, clearly not something he would wear at the store and generally not something you would wear on Christmas Eve. Mr. Monroe rotated his head slightly from the man to David as he studied them. Everyone remained silent and just allowed their eyes to communicate. After several long seconds, Mr. Monroe stepped back from the door and gestured them inside.

The room contained pleasing furnishings and soft light, mostly from the Christmas tree. Mr. Monroe gestured for them to sit on the sofa and they obediently complied. Mr. Monroe sat in a chair opposite them but at an angle so that he was not directly facing David, which David felt relieved about. Mr. Monroe was always a jolly sort whenever he had encountered him in the store, which is the only place David could remember encountering him, but here in his house, he seemed dour and somewhat sad.

"You don't have a crèche?" The man broke the silence of the room.

"Humph," Mr. Monroe grunted.

"It would lighten your earthly load and make the world problems insignificant," the man continued.

"Don't start with that crap. I know why you are here," The man shot back in such a hostile tone that it caught David off guard. David looked from the man to Mr. Monroe as he observed their hostile exchange, a completely different experience than at the funeral.

"Then you know that I am here for your best interests."

"My best interests!" Mr. Monroe's almost shouted, his irritation with the man showing. "You have no idea what my best interests might be! I suspect you are here for your own interests!"

The man maintained his calm composure. "My interests are not relevant here, only yours. Why else would we be here?"

"I don't need your interests or your concerns. I tried it your way and what did it get me? I don't need your nonsense. You should spend your time on someone else who might consider your Christian theories, Christmas, and the rest of it." Mr. Monroe seemed to gain energy as he spoke back to the man.

"You will find the peace you seek. Just let yourself accept what you know you want to accept," the man continued.

"Let me be miserable, will you? I am perfectly happy being the hardware guy in town, and I don't need anything that you have to offer. You might also try minding your own business. I don't need your Christmas or any of the rest of it. It's time for you to leave. I would suggest you do so now." Mr. Monroe's voice was firm and irritated. It was clear he did not want to have anymore of this conversation.

"Very well, but remember he loves you!" the man concluded.

The man rose and gestured to David to follow. David reached the door quickly and opened it, as he was anxious to leave before there was a fight between these two. As he did, he looked back at Mr. Monroe and thought once again about how little knowledge he possessed about people he knew. Johnny Bates, Becky, and now Mr. Monroe. He felt sorrow for Mr. Monroe, not in the same way as he had for Johnny or Becky, but rather sympathy that Mr. Monroe didn't share the same comfort that David had in his faith. He almost wanted to stay and speak with him more about having joy in his heart, but he knew that he had to follow the cue from his companion.

They made their way out the door. The man turned back to Mr. Monroe, who was standing in the doorway, and said, "By the way, that is a really nice Christmas tree!"

"It's a dead tree with lights on it," Mr. Monroe retorted.

"Merry Christmas and God bless you, Mr. Monroe!" the man responded as he and David exited the porch.

The door slammed behind them and the sound of it reverberated in David's ear in such a way that it echoed and escalated in volume until David had to cover his ears in pain. The volume continued to rise, which caused David to bend over and press his hands against his ears as hard as he could. Tears began to form in his tightly closed eyes.

And then the noise was suddenly gone and the night was completely silent. David realized he was no longer outside; he was in his room, in his bed. The man was nowhere to be seen and his room was just as he would have expected it to be, with nothing out of place. He got up and looked out into the hall. All was quiet, as one would expect in the middle of the night on Christmas Eve. Even his dad's snoring was on tempo and just as he would have expected. He looked up and down the hall for the man but it was empty and, except for the snoring, silent.

He went back into his room and sat on the bed. He thought that it must have been just a crazy dream, but he immediately knew that his adventures this night with his strange companion were not a dream, at least not in the normal context of dreams. He knew this was something beyond a dream. They didn't have the detail and logical continuity that he experienced tonight. So what had happened? He now really felt that somehow this was truly a type of intervention with Saint Joseph. Could it be possible? He knew that the evidence was now becoming overwhelming, especially since Becky had seen the man's footprints in the snow the other day.

Sleep finally overcame David's exhausted mind, and he fell into a deep and, fortunately for David, dreamless sleep.

The morning sun broke onto the snow-covered ground with a dazzle that seemed appropriate for celebrating this Christmas morning. David's sister Katy was staring at him when he awoke.

"David, don't you want to get up and see your presents? C'mon, everyone is waiting on you. Dad even did all the milking already."

David sat up with a start as he spun around to see that the time on his Big Ben alarm clock was 9:10. He could not believe he slept so late and missed milking the cows this morning! He sprang from bed and quickly dressed in jeans and a flannel shirt that he thought his mom would allow for Christmas morning.

Janet Edmonds was finishing up some homemade cinnamon rolls that were overtaking the house with their delicious aroma. David floated toward the kitchen on the fumes. As he walked past the front room, he caught sight of the family crèche, which caused him to contemplate his experience of the previous night. As he studied the figures, he knew in his heart that his strange visit with the man during the night had not been a dream, even though he had encountered it in a dreamlike situation. He knew that this had been something more. It had been real, or at least real in the sense that it was not just a dream to be dismissed in the

157

morning light. He pondered the Saint Joseph statue for a few moments before the smell of the rolls conspired to drag him the rest of the way into the kitchen.

"Merry Christmas, Mr. Sleepy!" His mom greeted him with a warm smile and a soft hug. "I'm amazed that you slept so late. That's not like you, especially on Christmas morning. You must have been enjoying some great dreams."

The mention of dreams caused David to look into his mother's eyes in fear that somehow she was in on the gig. "Dreams? What do you mean, dreams?"

"What? Well, nothing, just a comment about dreams. Why such a look of concern, David? You know sleeping late on Christmas morning, while unusual for a young person, is not a capital crime, at least not in this house. Now how about a cinnamon roll?" Janet Edmonds brushed past the strange anxiety displayed by her son and served him a still-warm homemade cinnamon roll and a fresh glass of raw milk from the dairy barn.

David took his roll, gave his mom a rather deadpan thank-you, and sat at the large dining table. As he ate in silence, his siblings, Katy, Judy, and Michael, were all bouncing off the walls with anticipation of opening the many gifts that waited so temptingly under the brightly lit Christmas tree. His mother watched her oldest son with continued concern. He was always the first to interact with his siblings on Christmas morning and get them even more frenzied than they already were, but not today. His mood was pensive, and he seemed absent somehow.

"David, hurry up so we can open the presents." Katy was begging. "I am sure that I got some really cool new clothes. I can't wait to try them on and you are holding up the show! Come see the tree!"

Her energy seemed to break David's spell and he smiled at Katy. "Sure, just let me finish this absolutely delicious cinnamon roll that Mom made, OK?"

"Hurry up, David!" Katy pleaded as she bounced back to the living room and the pile of brightly wrapped gifts.

Paul Edmonds entered the back door foyer and shouted a big Merry Christmas to everyone with a big smile on his face. "Hey, David, don't worry, I got all the cows milked and fed. At least I didn't have to buy *them* presents," he laughed. "What do you say we rip up some wrapping paper?"

A chorus of cheers went up from Katy, Judy, and Michael, as Mr. Edmonds made his way into the kitchen to plant a respectable kiss on his bride. David watched with quiet joy as he considered Johnny Bates and what his Christmas morning might be like, and Mr. Monroe, whose cold heart could not grasp any joy from this day. He then thought about his sweet Becky. She now almost seemed a stranger he did not really know, someone whose heart had a blind spot in it that was impervious to David. More than anything else, he wanted to go see her and look into her eyes, and somehow let her know that he knew of her pain. Not that he understood it, but that he was aware of it. Yes, that's what he wanted her to know. He could take her in his arms and absorb some of the torment she must feel on a day like today without her father there with her. He knew that Becky's family would be traveling to her uncle Dan's for Christmas Day. He felt he really needed to see her before she left.

"David, c'mon, hurry up with the roll, will you?" His mother was eyeing him with a bit of suspicion now, as his behavior today was as unusual as it had been for the past week.

David nodded and took the last bite of the roll and gulped down the milk. As he got up from the table, he realized that his behavior was causing concern for his mom, and even his dad was giving him some strange glances. So he decided he needed to be more like the David they were accustomed to, even though he felt like his life was now changed in ways that he could not yet really comprehend.

The Edmonds family was very organized on Christmas morning. Janet Edmonds was in charge of gift distribution and made sure that only one person at a time opened a gift that so the whole family could experience each person's gift receiving. The sequence was the first gift was opened by the youngest, Michael, and then it went chronologically along from there.

David was able to keep up his appearance of being himself as everyone oohed and aahed over the gifts as they were freed from their stubborn but colorful wrappings. His performance was convincing to everyone except Janet Edmonds, whose motherly instincts knew better. She kept a watchful eye on David as he went through the motions of feigned excitement. The children received toys and clothes and David got clothes, a new hunting knife, and a starter set of mechanic's tools from Sears that he had been wanting.

Much too soon the gift opening was complete and the children became very busy with their new toys and dolls. David was doing a less-than-convincing job of showing enthusiasm for his new tool set as he examined it.

"I think that's the one you wanted, son." Paul Edmonds commented in an almost inquisitive way that indicated he had expected a bit more excitement from David regarding this gift.

"Yes, Dad, it's great. Thanks so much. This is exactly the one I was asking for, and its Craftsman." David tried to put some fire in his response, but it was less than he had hoped.

Paul Edmonds now had excitement in his voice. "I think we should all take a short walk to shop for one more item."

"I think that is a capital idea. Everyone, grab your coats," Janet Edmonds added with her own air of excitement.

"C'mon, David, get your coat!" Little sister Judy seemed to be in on the secret, which was odd as she usually could not keep any kind of secret.

David watched as everyone grabbed coats and gloves as if he were watching a movie and was not really part of the action. His mind was still pondering the events of the previous night and his overpowering desire to see Becky.

"David, let's go, for Pete's sake!" Paul Edmonds was now a little irritated.

David gave a smile to his dad and jumped up to join the group. They marched across the driveway toward the machine shop. Every farm requires a workshop where all the various pieces of machinery can be maintained. A farmer has to be a hybrid of many trades to keep his operation going—mechanic, carpenter, welder, and construction worker. The shop was large with high ceilings that would accommodate a tractor or other large pieces of farm equipment.

Paul's grin was big enough to distort his face as he opened the main door to the shop and gestured for everyone to enter. Janet Edmonds took the rear position in the group and was literally pushing David forward ahead of her. David stepped into the large and cold shop and was immediately stopped in his tracks, mother or no mother pushing him.

There in front of him, topped by the most enormous bow David had ever seen and wrapped by a ridiculously large ribbon, was a 1955 Chevrolet Bel Air, the very one he had seen at the lot with Forrest Mandle just yesterday. Forrest had been cleaning it up for him! His parents had purchased this beautiful car for him! He was in a mild state of disbelief. With everything that had happened to him in the past few days, his focus had shifted from the desire for this car to much more significant issues. Still, he could not contain his immediate surprise and excitement upon seeing this beautiful machine.

"Actually, I had to get something to go with your tool set," his dad told him with a laugh.

"Let's go for a ride," shouted Katy. "This is so cool! You got a car for Christmas!"

"Dad, Mom, I don't know what to say. This is so, wow, so unexpected and I'm not even sure deserved," David said without taking his eyes from the shining chrome and freshly polished paint. He reached out and slid his hand along the tailfin and toward the front of the vehicle. He was enraptured with the reality of actually having this machine.

"Merry Christmas, son." Janet gave her son a hug while she, too, admired the car.

"You know, there is also a lot of responsibility with owning a car." Paul had to inject his fatherly counsel.

"Yes, of course, Dad. Thank you so much. I really don't know what to say. It's really almost too much." David continued to touch the car all the way to the front right headlight.

"How about it? Let's go for a ride!" Paul said.

"Ok, let's get this amazing ribbon off and take it for a spin," David agreed with glee.

With the joy that only a Christmas morning can deliver, the entire family squeezed into the two-door hardtop and slowly made their way out of the shop, down the driveway, and onto the road. David was most cautious as he maneuvered the powerful V-8. The road was completely deserted, as it appeared no one else had yet ventured out on this Christmas morning. David could hardly believe what he was experiencing. Yes, he had wanted this car and he knew his parents might be considering it, but he had always mentally prepared himself for something less. He really wasn't sure he deserved it.

Without any real idea of where to go, he soon found himself driving down Main Street, the same street he had walked just last night, or so it had seemed. He instinctively turned toward the Presbyterian Church and slowed down as they drove by it. This building now took on a completely different aspect to him; his mind was drawn from the pleasure of this drive to the experience of the funeral for Mr. Marston. He once again felt the pain of seeing Becky there, and he was now more convinced than ever that whatever happened to him last night was not a dream. The emotional pain of having this now-shared experience with Becky overshadowed what suddenly seemed like shallow joy regarding being the owner of a car.

As he was swept into his thoughts about the night before, the family fawned over the car and how nice it was and made jokes about David having to take his siblings wherever they wanted to go instead of having Janet be their chauffeur.

Without really considering it, he found himself steering the car toward the Bates' residence. He was not even thinking about the turns or direction of the car; it was as if the car had taken on the role of the driver. David felt as if he were just a passenger in his new car. The Edmonds family was busy enjoying the ride in the shiny Bel Air and did not take any notice of where they were headed.

David was almost surprised to see that the house was just as it looked the night before, or at least as he had seemed to dream it. As he looked at the faded house exterior, the unkempt yard with the broken fence, the dirty windows, and the roof in need of some care, he could also see the Christmas tree and its lights through the dirty windows. He slowed to almost a stop as he peered at the gloomy house with an almost obsessive curiosity. Here he was with his family, who probably knew nothing about the Bates family, and he had almost intimate knowledge of how sparse their Christmas morning was proceeding.

"David, is there something about this house that interests you?" Paul Edmonds, who was riding in the front passenger seat, quipped while also looking at the house to see what was so interesting. "Isn't this where the widow Bates lives?"

"It's Mrs. Bates and her son, Johnny. They live here alone," David responded.

"Isn't Johnny in your class?" Janet Edmonds spoke from the back seat.

"Yes, he is in my class," David responded flatly.

They slowly pulled away from the Bates' residence, but David tried to maintain his view of it via the small, round rearview mirror. He found himself lost in his memories of the previous night's strange visits.

A short drive later, David found himself passing in front of the Monroe house. It also appeared as the night before, neat and well kept, with the small Christmas tree defiantly signaling the holiday from inside. David slowed the Chevy again as he rolled past the house and studied it, for what he was not sure, maybe just affirmation of his experience of the night before.

"Hey, that's Bob Monroe's house. I know his store was really busy just before Christmas, so I bet he is having a great holiday!" Paul Edmonds commented. Paul stole a glance toward David, as this pattern of driving was not what he expected from a teenager in his first car for a first drive. No one else commented on this part of the route, and David was past the house in just a minute.

"Can't this car go fast?" Michael shouted from the back seat. "Why are you going so slow anyway?"

David smiled at his comment. "OK, Michael, we can go faster, probably a lot faster." David pressed the accelerator and the car lurched forward with a jerk that startled not only Michael but David as well. He was surprised by the muscle of the small-block V-8 tucked under the hood. Katy chortled with a giggle at the quick jump of the car.

Janet Edmonds was startled but not so amused. "Now, David, you be careful! You need to drive safely, especially with so little driving experience."

"Don't worry, Mom. I won't do anything stupid." David reassured his mom and gave a visual nod to his dad.

The rest of the drive was strictly for pleasure. The family commented on the various features of the car, the colors, the sounds, comfort of the seats, and everything in between. The drive finally concluded with everyone congratulating and hugging David and with David hugging and thanking his mom and dad.

"I would like to drive over to Becky's house and show her the car before she leaves for her uncle's for Christmas dinner. Would that be OK?" David asked his mom as he was giving her a thank-you hug.

"Do you think that it would be OK with Mrs. Marston for you to show up on Christmas Day?" Janet Edmonds narrowed her eyes as she looked straight at David.

"Yes, Mom, Mrs. Marston loves me!" David responded with a lighthearted laugh.

"Well, OK, but be sure to be back here to help with our dinner. After all, you did miss the morning milking!" Janet's tone was one of approval and a little bit of jest.

David committed to be back on time and quickly jumped back into the Chevy. He slowly maneuvered out of the driveway and onto the county road again. Although he was anxious to see Becky and he knew that he had a limited timeline to see her before her annual Christmas departure, he found himself once again driving toward the Bates' home. He could not decide why, but he knew that he had to view it again.

He also routed his new Chevy by the Monroe residence. Although there was nothing new at either residence, his mind found that it could not resist the journey back to his visits of the night before. The new awareness of these people's lives that he had never even remotely considered previously now bothered him profoundly. Why had the man taken him on such visits and what did that have to do with his earlier strange visits from this man. He did not know these answers, but his fear of the man was metastasizing into a fear of his own unawareness of other people's lives. He realized he was uncomfortable with being disrupted from his own cozy environs. He shuddered as he drove away from the Monroe house and toward Becky's house.

He rolled the Chevy slowly up in front of Becky's house. If this had been the week before, he would have been bouncing out of the car with glee to show it off to his best girl. Now the heavy weight of having been a strange witness at Mr. Marston's funeral was almost suffocating the normal enthusiasm for the car from his soul. He turned the key and listened as the engine came to an obedient stop and silence filled the car. He suddenly did not want to leave the car and face Becky and somehow hide the fact from her that he now knew so much more of her inner sorrow. How did she overcome it with such grace and what appeared to be an absence of effort? Winter slowly crept its way into the car, as the stopped engine caused the heat to quickly dissipate. David could see the translucent fog of his breath and realized he had been sitting there too long. He knew he had to decide whether to leave or do the right thing and speak with Becky.

His flamboyant parking space right in front of the house did not leave much choice but for Becky to see him. Thus, before David could make the manly decision to march in and see her, she was rapping on the window with a giggle and a smile. David quickly rolled down the driver's window to face Becky.

"What are you doing sitting here? Is this *yours*?" Becky's wide eyes studied the interior. "I couldn't tell who was parked in front of our house until Roger said it was you. What are you doing, silly?"

"Becky!" David looked into her face as if he had never seen her before. He studied her delicate features, small, slightly upturned nose, large almond-shaped eyes, and beautiful smile. He looked for the face of the girl he had seen the night before, the overwhelming sadness that he could not expel from his mind. The bright eyes and sweet smile beguiled any evidence of the sadness he was looking for in that face.

"Yes, it's me. Who did you expect to come out of my house? Honestly, are you OK? You didn't steal this car, did you?" she said with a laugh.

"No, of course I didn't steal it. It was my Christmas gift from my parents. Can you believe it?" David said.

"Really, wow, that is quite a gift. You must be really excited. Are you going to give me a ride or what? You know I have to leave for Uncle Dan's in just a few minutes." Becky was relieved that David seemed OK.

David opened his door and got out so he could put his arms around Becky. He gave her a hug and a kiss that acknowledged his newfound respect for this wonderful girl. Becky didn't know why David had suddenly turned into such an affectionate man, but she didn't complain. David felt as if there was a silent communication passing between them, an energy that was beyond a mating ritual. It seemed to him that Becky was also feeling this elevated state of emotion. He held and kissed her for a long minute, and as he pulled his face back from hers, he gazed into her large eyes. She returned the loving gaze with an acknowledgment of the unspoken newfound depth of feeling between them.

When they finally broke their embrace, David took Becky's arm and helped her into the car, where she took her rightful place in the middle of the front seat next to her boy, although he now seemed more like her man. David spun the car to life and they both squealed with delight as the Chevy found its way back into the street for a quick Christmas morning cruise around Seltice Falls.

They wound around town at slow speeds just enjoying each other's company and the freedom that only having your own car can deliver. Being Christmas morning, there wasn't anyone around to honk at and show off the new wheels to but that could wait for another day. David found them passing the Presbyterian Church, and he could not help but bring the car to a stop in front.

"This is your church, isn't it?" David asked while keeping his eyes fixed on the church.

"Yes, of course it is. You know that already, silly, and why are we stopped here?" Becky gave a slight laugh.

"I was here last night, with that man." David said, almost to himself and without thinking about his passenger.

"What? That man, you mean, the Saint Joseph guy?" Becky immediately took a serious tone.

"Yes, I know this is really weird, but we were at your dad's funeral," David said without taking his view from the front of the church.

"What! David, you are scaring me. What are you talking about, my dad's funeral? That is not funny." Becky's tone turned angry.

David now turned to Becky. "I can't explain it. It was like in a dream but it was real, not a dream at all. The man took me to this church and when we went in, we were at your dad's funeral. I know how this must sound but, Becky,

I swear it happened. I sat in the front pew with you, Roger, and your mom." David now kept his eyes fixed on Becky.

"Stop it, David! I think this has gone far enough. Why are you even speaking of that horrible day?" Becky looked away from David as she spoke.

"Sorry. What I really wanted to tell you is how sorry I am for your suffering and sorrow from that day and the loss of your dad. I never really had any appreciation for what you had to experience. I'm not trying to weird you out or anything. I only wanted to tell you about it so that I could somehow try and empathize with you." David felt helpless with his pleading. He could see Becky did not want to hear anything about this part of her past.

"Please take me home now," Becky said coldly.

"Becky, please, I didn't mean to cause you any pain, but I really did have this happen to me last night."

"What was I wearing?" Becky looked back up at David, tears welling in her eyes.

"What?" David was caught off-balance with this question.

"What was I wearing?" Becky repeated.

David realized that she was trying to believe him, so he followed her lead. "You were wearing a black lace kind of a dress with a small black hat that also had a lace veil. You had the veil pulled over your face, but I could still see through it enough to see the sadness in your eyes. Your shoes were black patent leather and you were scrunching a small white handkerchief in your hands, a tear-stained handkerchief. The handkerchief had a dainty pink border with small red flowers embroidered on the inside." David continued to describe Roger's suit and tie, as well as what Mary Marston was wearing. He also described the church flowers, what the minister was wearing, and other details of the church that day.

"How could you know all that, especially about the handkerchief? I have kept that handkerchief hidden in a secret place ever since that day. How could you know about it?" Becky gave David a look as if she were now with a stranger.

"I told you, I was there last night. I don't know how, but the man and I were there. I don't know why I was there either." David almost shrugged as he looked away from Becky's icy stare. "Somehow we went back in time. I guess it was some kind of vision or maybe it was dream, but not a dream, because it was too real. Even though I cannot explain it, there is no way this was just something I dreamt about in my sleep. Sleep dreams are different."

"David, I'm scared. I don't understand what is happening to you and all these strange visions and hallucinations. I don't like that somehow I am being pulled into them, either. I think you better take me home. I don't think I can absorb any more of your bizarre experiences, and my mom will be anxious to leave for my uncle Dan's." Becky kept her gaze straight ahead and did not look toward David.

"I understand, Becky. But I want you to know that I didn't just make this up to scare you or make you uncomfortable. I just needed to share this with someone. I don't have anyone else I can speak to about it. But I truly did not mean to frighten you." David started the car, pulled away from the curb, and made his way back toward Becky's house.

Becky softened her demeanor by the time the Chevy rolled up to her house, where Mrs. Marston was clearly watching from the front room. "David, it's obvious there is more going on here than just you having visions or hallucinations. I certainly don't understand it either, but I know you would not make up something like this, and I want to be there for you. You clearly had some kind of unique but real visit to the past, because there is no way you could have all that knowledge of my dad's funeral otherwise. Let's get together tomorrow, OK?" She smiled and gave David as much of a departing kiss as her mother's glare would allow.

As their lips parted, David's expression of affection could not be restrained. "I love you, Becky." David found the "L" word slipping out as he watched her exit the car and make her way to the house. Becky's serious face changed into a grin as she walked toward her front door.

David maneuvered the Chevy back onto the street and started off again. Although he knew he should be heading for home, he found himself once again cruising toward the Bates' home. The car rolled by the house slowly as David studied it once again. He was not sure what he was looking for, but he felt he would know it if he saw it. He almost expected to see the Saint Joseph man looking out from the dirty front window, but of course no one was there, just the lonely Christmas tree. He was almost overcome with empathy and sadness for Johnny. He wanted to somehow let him know that he had a new understanding of things. He wanted to reach out to Johnny to show him some kindness, but he did not really know how to accomplish that. He continued down the street and stopped at the end of the block. He sat with the engine idling and looked around the neighborhood. The buildings, streets, trees, and sidewalks seemed surprisingly new this morning, as if a veil had been lifted and the world, even his familiar Seltice Falls, was a place he was visiting for the first time. He wanted to take in every detail and ponder this new town before him.

The Chevy also fell under his examination and appraisal. How was it that the dice of life had landed with blessings on him while others got a much more difficult path? The Chevy seemed to look back at him with a level of scorn at his zealous coveting of such a machine. Others, people he knew, did not even have reason to celebrate this day.

He was not sure how long he had sat there, but as he pondered the rapid sequence of things that had befallen him, he felt an awakening start to emerge. He knew that all of this was happening within his mind, but there was a physical sensation to it as well. It was as if he were growing physically lighter, to such a degree as to almost float from the seat of the car. The sensation started to bubble into ideas and finally a type of revelation. His mind began to realize that it was not too late to consider those with less fortune. He could start today to embrace them and reach out to them to share some of his joy and good fortune.

In this new state of awareness, he put the car in gear and slowly released the clutch. The car lurched forward and started down the street. As the car made its way in the direction of his parent's house, he thought about his life as if he were looking in from the outside as an objective observer. It was not hard to conclude that he had been the beneficiary of a multitude of blessings and good fortune. He realized he wanted to be at home to hug his mom and dad, and even his siblings.

"Well, did Becky like the car?" his dad immediately asked as David bounced into the kitchen from the back stoop.

"Becky?" David was so engrossed in his newfound life assessment that he almost forgot why he was out driving in the first place, but he quickly recovered. "Oh yeah, she loved it, of course."

Now that he was standing right in front of his dad, the urge to hug him diminished. Hugging his dad was not something he did, ever. Instead, he decided to ask him a question. "Dad, did you know Mr. Marston, Becky's dad?"

"What?" Paul Edmonds was expecting some gleeful teenage banter about the joys of the new car. He was caught off guard with this strange query.

"You know, Becky's dad, did you know him?" David persisted.

"Dick Marston? Of course I knew him. Did something happen with you and Becky to prompt this out-of-the-blue question?" David knew that Paul Edmonds's furrowed brow was not a good sign when engaging in such a conversation.

"No, nothing like that. I guess having such a great Christmas with a loving family like I have made me think about what Becky must have suffered when her dad died. I just never really thought about it until today." David was not going to bring up the dream or the man to his dad.

"I see. Well, of course, I'm glad to hear your appreciation of your family. It takes a level of maturity to achieve that. I knew Dick Marston. Seems like everybody in town knew Dick. He was a good man. He and I worked together on a couple of projects to help the needy kids in the county. Dick was always there to help kids. He was a scout leader, helped with the Toys for Tots drive every year, and had a really nice family. Of course, you know that better than me." While looking out the window, Paul continued. "That was really a blow for a little town like Seltice Falls, having Dick die in an accident like that. I can tell you it was a shocker. I know people still talk about it, and him. I did not know his family that well, but I know they are good people and all highly respected in the community. Did Becky bring this up to you?"

"No, Becky didn't mention anything. Like I said, I just contemplated my own life and how I have not had to really deal with anything remotely like that kind of situation." David looked his dad in the eye, and although he knew he was pressing now, he asked, "Did you attend the funeral?"

"The funeral? Why yes, both your mother and I went there to pay our respects. Why would you ask about that?" Paul's brow went into furrow overdrive.

David was not really mentally prepared for this level of discussion. "Well, you know, it makes me feel better to know that my family was there. I know I didn't go. Why did just you and Mom go?"

"David, we knew that the Presbyterian Church would be packed to the rafters for that funeral, and we felt it would be better to have your mother and I represent our family and not take up church space that might be better for other families to attend." Paul seemed to relax his inquisitive look a bit. "Why don't we save anymore of this conversation for another time? After all, it is Christmas day and I can smell a really nice dinner that your mom is working on for today's feast."

David nodded in agreement and then without hesitation stepped toward his dad and gave him an unexpected hug. Paul tensed his body at first but relaxed into acceptance of his son's embrace, and for the first time in many years, Paul Edmonds had to blink back tears. In that moment, he experienced a father's joy at knowing his son was a butterfly springing from the cocoon of childhood to the rigors of manhood with the strong kind of character a parent longs for in their child.

David hugged his mom next, which was easier because it was not as foreign as hugging his dad. His mom instinctively returned the hug. David gushed his thanks for the car and his mom just hugged him back with a heartfelt, "You're welcome."

There was no more talk of Mr. Marston that day as they all enjoyed the feast that Janet Edmonds had prepared for them: a sugar ham, green beans, baked potatoes, and many other fabulous side dishes.

After dinner the family battled through a game of Clue, a round of Parcheesi, and David managed to checkmate his dad in a hotly contested round of chess.

As David helped his mom clean up the last of the dishes with the still-lingering aroma of the cobbler dessert in the air, he took the opportunity to query her because his dad was in the living room with the other children. "Mom, do you know the Bateses? I mean, Johnny and his mom?"

"Of course I do. You know they go to our church. Isn't Johnny in your class at school?" Janet Edmonds curiosity was up.

"Yeah, I know Johnny. Well, sort of know him. He kind of keeps to himself and doesn't seem to have any friends. You know, he is kind of weird, too." David said.

"I'm not surprised with the tough life he has had. His no-good drunk of a dad left them when Johnny was just a toddler. Whenever I see Johnny at mass, I feel sorry for him. I don't really know him, of course, but I know enough of his background. His mom isn't the model citizen either, but she has had her crosses to bear also." Janet paused to look at her son quizzically. "Listen to me, speaking so poorly about people on Christmas Day! Why the sudden interest in Johnny Bates?"

"Well, I keep thinking about how lucky I am to have great parents, a comfortable life, and, well heck, even great siblings." David did not want to expose too much of his real interest to his mom, but his inner urge was to shout, "Mom, I was at their house last night and saw how poorly they live!" He didn't do this, of course, but the words felt like they were prying for escape.

"David, are you OK?" Janet Edmonds's motherly instincts were sharp enough to know that this conversation on Christmas Day, a Christmas Day when her son had just gotten the biggest gift of his life, was somehow out of place. She was now studying David's downcast face for some sign of what was behind the conversation.

"I'm fine. It's just getting such a fantastic gift made me think about things, that's all." David did not want to talk about it any further with someone as instinctively intuitive as his mom.

David gave his mom a hug that was intended to provide reassurance that his altruistic motives really did spring forth from nothing more than the special gift.

"Maybe that is the best thing about such a gift. It also shows a level of maturity that makes me proud of my son," Janet said softly as she extended the hug.

"Mom, would you mind if I took the Chevy out for a drive?" David was not sure where this came from. It seemed that somehow his subconscious had short-circuited straight to his brain.

"Now? Don't you want to relax and play some of the new games with the rest of the family?" Janet Edmonds was now a bit irritated and somewhere in her mind, the question of whether getting this boy his own car was such a good idea start to sprout.

"I just feel like a drive. Maybe I'll stop by Mike's house. You know he will really like the car." David's subconscious had not yet relinquished its control of his mouth.

Mrs. Edmonds reluctantly gave a wave of her hand in a clear indication of her tacit approval of his request.

David piloted the Bel Air back onto the county blacktop and toward Mike Glatter's house. Mike's family lived on a small farm that was not a business farm but more of a hobby of his dad's. Mr. Glatter worked at the local grange supply store but enjoyed being a gentleman farmer. Mike did not share his enthusiasm for the micro farming but contributed his part nonetheless.

"David, you have got to be shitting me! You got this car for Christmas?" Mike almost shouted as David showed off the car in the Glatter driveway. "This is the coolest Christmas gift I have ever seen, man!"

They performed the obligatory examination of the car's engine, trunk, and interior and, of course, the radio. As they did their audit of the car, David realized that he had not even taken the time to do this function at home with his dad, something he would normally always do on any kind of a vehicle.

Without too many perfunctory inspection practices, they jumped in the car and headed down the road. As any young boys would, they tried all the various functions, including squealing the rear tires on the pavement and jamming gears as they raced out of town on the main highway. They criss-crossed the town's meager streets, waving at anyone that would notice these two testosterone-laden boys.

Without any discussion, David pulled up in front of the Bates' house once again.

"What the hell are we stopping here for, David?" Mike spoke while studying the ugly house in front of them.

"Just a minute," David said flatly as he exited the car and walked up the crumbling, ice-strewn sidewalk.

Mike's wide eyes watched David in confusion as he approached the front door of the Bates' house. After knocking, David stood patiently until the door creaked open and Johnny Bates appeared. Mike could see David speaking and motioning toward the car, while a confused and clearly skeptical Johnny looked from David to the big Chevy at the curb. Mike was bewildered at what his friend was up to, as neither of them had really ever been that familiar with the odd Johnny Bates, much less ever visited his ugly house.

Johnny started to nod and his face started to soften, not into a smile but more of a suspicious smirk. He was now looking more at the Chevy and less at David as David continued to speak, his fogged breath clearly visible against the cold night air.

Johnny then turned back into the house for about thirty seconds while David stood on the porch waiting for something, the front door still ajar. Johnny reappeared with his winter coat, not much more than a ragged secondhand thing, and both he and David headed toward the car. Without any conscious thought, Mike's eyes opened wide as he observed this strange interaction between his best friend and Johnny.

Just when Mike thought this could not get any stranger, David opened the driver's door and, with a gesture of his hand, told Johnny to go ahead and drive!

"Really? Are you sure, David? Isn't this your new car?" Johnny studied David's face, trying to read the motivation behind this unexpected encounter.

"Sure, please take her for a spin." David was smiling broadly as he continued to gesture for Johnny to take the helm.

Mike could only watch; he was literally speechless as he watched Johnny slide into the driver's seat and begin to touch the coveted controls. David took his place in the middle of the back seat and leaned over the front bench seat to give piloting instructions. Mike looked at David with an expression that clearly said, "What in the hell are you doing?!" David only broadened his smile and winked at Mike. Mike looked back at Johnny.

"Hi, Mike," Johnny said without looking at him.

"Uh, yeah, hi, Johnny," Mike responded weakly. Mike was trying to figure out what the practical joke was here. He and David had pulled plenty of practical jokes on folks over the years, but he was always in on the plan prior to its execution. This was a complete mystery. Maybe the joke was on him. Mike definitely did not like being the victim of one of David's jokes, but thus far the evidence seemed to point in that direction.

David watched as Johnny caressed the steering wheel and the gearshift knob, and then lightly brushed his hand across the instrument cluster in the dashboard. Johnny was in a dreamlike state as he absorbed this most unusual experience. His head pivoted around the interior, drinking it all in like a coveted, sought-after cognac. After what seemed like a lengthy peruse of the car, Johnny finally reached for the ignition and spun the key hard to the right. The big V-8 responded with muscular growl. He gave a quick glance and a sly smile toward Mike, who was watching all this in a muted, mouth-agape stare. It was not lost on Mike that *he* hadn't been invited to drive yet!

Johnny feathered the throttle and the Bel Air made its way around town with David pointing and giving him instructions as they went. Mike kept looking between David and Johnny trying to unravel the joke here, but so far it was eluding him. After a couple of rotations around several blocks, Johnny's face split into a big smile, bad teeth and all. Mike saw that David seemed to be in a state of delight at Johnny's joy in driving this wonderful machine.

"Let's stop at the house right there." David was pointing as he gave directions to Johnny. Mike stayed in stunned silence and continued studying his friend, who kept looking back at him with a silly wink and grin.

The car rolled up in front of Bob Monroe's house. Johnny killed the engine as instructed by David and followed David as he jumped from the car. David signaled to Mike to follow them while maintaining the silly grin. Mike decided that this must be part of the joke on Johnny, and he smiled to himself thinking that he was about to see the punch line. Mike was thinking that David had really put this one together carefully, and he was starting to wonder if the car really belonged to David at all. Mike jumped from the car still hoping that this elaborate joke, if indeed it was a joke, was not going to lead to his embarrassment.

David led the way to the front door and without hesitation proceeded to knock loudly. In less than half a minute, Bob Monroe was standing in the open doorway with a puzzled look on his face.

"What is it, boys?" he said in his practiced customer service voice.

"Merry Christmas, Mr. Monroe!" David blurted out.

"Uh, Merry Christmas . . . David, isn't it?" Mr. Monroe responded automatically.

"We just wanted to stop by and wish you a great Christmas Day! I hope you had a great day!" David continued.

"Are you putting me on?"

"No sir, we are as sincere as we can be. We hope you had a fantastic Christmas Day!" David kept up the enthusiasm.

"Well, OK, then, why don't you guys come in from out of the cold. Let's have a drink! Hot chocolate, of course!" Mr. Monroe's skepticism melted, and he gestured to the boys to come into the house.

Mike was studying all of this while trying to analyze what the joke might be, or if indeed there was a joke somewhere. It seemed to have gone too far to kick in a punch line at this point. Mike knew that both his dad and Mr. Edmonds would kick their collective butts if they pulled some kind of embarrassing joke on Bob Monroe. Mike decided to play along and find out later from David what in the hell they were up to on this sojourn.

They introduced themselves as Mr. Monroe made them some hot chocolate and fixed himself a scotch on the rocks. They chatted about high school, and Mr. Monroe seemed to open up in a way they would never have expected, as they knew him only from his hardware store. As they told funny stories of high school antics, Bob Monroe was drawn into their youthful exuberance and could not help but tell some hilarious stories about his youth and prank exploits from the past. Mike and Johnny were drawn into the energy between David and Mr. Monroe, and soon they were both talking and laughing as they sipped their steaming drinks.

The enchantment of the room was broken when Johnny realized he needed to get home or his mom would be really worried. The boys all agreed that it was time to go, as they had exhausted their hot chocolates and the best of their stories. They shook hands with Mr. Monroe, who clearly had enjoyed the evening, and headed for the now-frigid car.

To Mike's ultimate surprise, David dropped him off first before giving Johnny a ride to his house. Mike only shook his head as his friend drove away with this strange boy. This entire episode with Johnny Bates remained quite the mystery. Mike laughed out loud as he walked toward his house and uttered, "Johnny Bates? Ha, what the hell is the joke here, David?"

David and Johnny chatted like old friends as they drove toward Johnny's humble house. Johnny remained skeptical of this strange endearment from these people, but he could not find any obvious fault with the evening's encounters.

David was buoyant as he arrived home. It was late and his siblings were already in bed, having exhausted themselves after a hectic Christmas Day. David hugged his mom and dad, who exchanged quizzical looks of surprise regarding their son's unexpected behavior. David chatted about his ride with Mike, but he did not disclose his stop at the Bates' home or to see Mr. Monroe, as he was not prepared to try to explain it. He did not even understand it himself yet. After visiting quietly in front of the fireplace with his parents for a short time, his human frailty caught up with him and he found his way to bed, where he was asleep in a matter of minutes.

He was sitting alone in the front pew. The now hauntingly familiar crèche was straight in front of him. He wanted to pray but the familiar rote prayers of his Catholic indoctrination did not seem to carry any punch or the weight that he needed this morning. Instead he found himself speaking to God in a way that he seldom did. He had finished his chores with his dad, breakfast with his family, and then once again was off in the Chevy. This morning he did not go to the haunts of yesterday from his dreams, if they were dreams. He came to this quiet church sanctuary, where he felt he could absorb something from the "holy" atmosphere inside. He watched the Saint Joseph statue carefully for some kind of motion, sign, or something else not expected by those without paranormal experiences to reference. The statue remained static and obedient to its ceramic genesis.

After some quiet moments, he found himself speaking aloud, quietly, but aloud. He was addressing Saint Joseph, asking him to clarify what this was all about and why he, David Edmonds, had been chosen for this experience. He was mature enough to recognize the beneficial positive aspects of his recent experiences, but he could not seem to coalesce them into anything useful to himself or anything that he could do.

"It doesn't work that way." A voice erupted behind him.

David jumped as this voice broke into the relative silence of his spoken thoughts. He spun around to see who was behind him.

"It doesn't work that way." Father Donovan had silently taken up a seat directly behind him.

"Father! I did not hear you come in!" David was embarrassed at being caught in this awkward and somewhat disarming situation. "What do you mean? What doesn't work what way?"

"You are asking God for some magical message of what to do. That is not how God works. If he did, there would be no free will for us to mess things up like we do. You see, son, God always shines a light in the right direction, but it competes with other lights of this world and the evil one. It is up to us to decipher the right path and make independent and free decisions of choosing that path. Generally, in our material world, the path of God appears to be less appealing, but in fact it will turn out to be the most satisfying and fulfilling path over the long run." Father Donovan continued while David watched and listened. "The really good news is that God never stops shining his light. No matter how far from his desired path we might wonder, we can always find our way back to him and his love."

"You remember what I told you in confession?" David was not sure he could even mention this outside of the veil of the confessional.

"Yes, David, but that is not important. Regardless of your experiences, in however you interpret it, God is shining his light for you. You just have to figure out which direction to go to follow it. Son, if you were experiencing some kind of heavenly apparition, it does not change your earthly duties or challenges, and actually, it probably increases them as you have been chosen for an elevated role in your mortal state.

Not an easy assignment for anyone. Even if your visions are only some kind of manifestations in your own mind, your duties here on this earth still remain the same. Understand?"

"I guess." David shrugged. "I'm really confused by all of this, and I'm upset that I have to be the one that is put in this spot. I would prefer that God, Saint Joseph, or whoever it is would just come out and make it plain as to what it is they want!"

The priest broke into a loud laugh that was sudden enough and at sufficient volume to violate the normal still-ness of the semi-dark church interior. He spoke as his laugh continued into his speech in a soft form of a chuckle. "David, if faith was as simple as God giving such specifics, it would no longer be faith, it would be some kind of branch of phys-iological science. You have to take your experiences and superimpose them with the morals that your parents, church, and community have instilled in you. Then, and only then, can you decide what you need to do. The fact that you are sit-ting in church on the day after Christmas on your Christmas break tells me that you already know there is something more for you to do. I guess you could view it as a crappy deal for you, but on the other hand, what a blessing to have such enlightenment. Either way, that's the deal." The priest paused to study David's face. David kept his gaze forward toward the crèche and did not look at the priest.

"Why don't you take some time alone to pray about it? That would seem a good idea since you're already here, right? I suspect that is why you came here in the first place." The priest paused again for a moment. "All right, David, I'm going to let you chat with God for a while. Good luck with your decisions."

David kept staring ahead as Father Donovan rose, left the pew, genuflected, and made his way toward the back of the church. As David watched the Saint Joseph statue, he noticed that the footfalls of the departing priest were all but silent. In such a quiet place, this did not seem realistic. He broke from his fixation on the Saint Joseph statue to turn to watch the priest leave the sanctuary.

After all that had happened this Christmas, David was not surprised to see that the figure slowly and silently walking toward the rear exit of the church was not Father Donovan at all but the man, with his long hair, scruffy beard, and tunic. David watched in silence, strangely without fear or dread now but with wonder as the man walked, or floated, toward the church door. Just before the man reached the door, he stopped and slowly turned around, his vision directed straight to David. The man's face was now one of contentment and maybe even joy as he gave David a slight smile and a barely discernable nod. He held his gaze with David for only a second or two before slowly turning again to make his exit through the double doors of the church, the doors that seemed to open effortlessly for him and close silently. David knew these doors all too well to think that they could behave so well in a silent church interior.

Just as the man disappeared, David jumped from his seat and sprinted after him. Without a doubt, he knew that the image of the priest was really this strange man speaking directly to him about faith, experiences, life, and what he should do now. He did not need to contemplate how the man had appeared as Father Donovan. What difference did that make now after all the strange events of the last couple of weeks? David wanted to grab the man and find the final answers to his mysteries.

It seemed that he reached the back of the church and the double doors in mere microseconds. He grabbed the long, ornate gold-plated handles and swung the right door open with such force that it knocked him off balance and he had to step back to steady himself.

Reorienting his balance, he charged out the open door about three or four seconds after the man had exited the same doorway. He dashed out onto the large front stoop of the church to completely empty front steps, sidewalk, and parking area. David stopped on the top step to study the area around the front of the church and up and down the adjoining streets. The man had vanished, apparently into thin air.

David started to think that the man had not only exited the church but exited his life as well. He felt alone. He knew he could not completely share these experiences, not even with Becky. He did not want to risk alienating her with his bizarre stories, even if she could see that there was more to them than just his imagination. In the cold December air, David sat down on the top step of the church stoop and contemplated his situation.

"David?" It was again the familiar voice of Father Donovan.

"Father!" David jumped up and sprang toward the priest, who was standing below him on the sidewalk. David's face broke into a broad smile as he literally lunged toward the surprised priest, who could not have known that David assumed that the man had returned.

"Everything all right, son?" Father Donovan stepped back from the anxious boy who reached out and grabbed the priest's forearms as he approached him. "David?"

As David's eyes met with Father Donovan, it was clear that this was the earthly priest and not the man. David shrank back and released his grip on the priest's forearms. Regardless of his effort to restrain them, tears started to well up in his eyes, tears of fear, tears of confusion, and tears of disappointment at not being able to speak with the man again. "Sorry, Father, I guess I got carried away. It has been a really strange Christmas for me this year. I guess that is putting it mildly." David was surprised that this comment actually fostered a slight smile on his face.

"Sure, David. Is everything all right? Can I help you with anything?" The priest paused for a moment as he studied David's face. "Say, is this related to our discussion in the confessional? You know I can't speak about it outside of the confessional, but I do want to make sure you are all right."

David hesitated and looked down to avoid the parental stare of Father Donovan. "Yes, it is a little bit related. I'm just a bit confused right now, but I will be OK."

The priest's scowling face gave a slight nod. "All right, well, come see me if you want to discuss, OK?"

"Sure." David gave a forced smile, turned away from the priest, and started to walk back toward his car. He expected the priest to call after him, but Father Donovan did not oblige. David entered his Bel Air interior, his new sanctuary from his muddled world. He roared the Chevy to life, partly to put some mental barrier between himself and Father Donovan but also to warm the car from the December cold.

Becky was glad to see David pull up in front of her house, although it was unusual for him to visit unannounced. David was always very considerate of Becky's mom's expectations about a boyfriend. She felt the butterflies gathering in her stomach as she anticipated seeing David again, even though she was still troubled by their last conversation about her dad's funeral. She watched from the living room window but kept a low profile, as she did not want to be seen pining for him this much through the plate glass. To Becky's frustration, David stayed seated in the Bel Air with the motor running. He seemed to be just staring ahead without purpose, like a toy with a low battery. She tried to view him at a sharper angle to try to get a glimpse of his face and see if could read his expression. To her chagrin, she could not get a proper angle to see his face, at least not enough of his face to read it.

Finally, the Chevy coughed to a stop and the steaming exhaust halted its exit from the dual pipes. Still David sat almost motionless in the driver's seat. Becky kept her vigil from behind the protective warmth of the living room plate-glass window. As the Northern Idaho winter crept into the Bel Air's interior, it roused David from his meditation and he finally broke from his reverie and slowly emerged from the car. Becky watched him as he walked around the car and up the sidewalk toward the front door. His face was a mask, not like the bouncing boy she had come to know and love. She knew David had depth beyond a careless teenager, that was one thing she loved about him, but this was different. David's deep ruminations were generally reserved for considerations of science, space travel, and the marvels of physics, not the deep furrows in his face that she observed on this day. It was as if his soul was troubled to such an extent as to now have taken up residence on his exterior.

She watched him disappear from view as he stepped up on the porch to the door. Anticipating an immediate knock, she began to get angry as David was apparently just standing on the porch without knocking. After an exasperating few seconds, Becky went to the door and opened it.

David jumped back as the door opened and Becky stood before him. She gave him a stern but worried look as their eyes met.

"David, what are you doing out here? It's freezing." Becky held her gaze with him.

"Sorry, can we talk?" David said flatly.

"Yes, yes, of course. Now will you please come in?" Becky grabbed his arm and pulled him into the warmth of the house.

She led him into the living room and guided him to a sofa where they could sit together. She was hoping to at least get snuggles from her troubled boyfriend today.

"Hey, lover boy. Heard you got a nice set of wheels. Man, now that's what I call a Christmas gift. I'm surprised you're not cruising the entire county, maybe even hitting the streets of Spokane." Roger Marston barked from the kitchen doorway.

David only nodded and smiled. His enthusiasm for the car was being engulfed by a muddle of guilt, confusion, and a little bit of fear. "Yeah, thanks, Roger."

To Roger this seemed like a ridiculously meager response to his inquiry about the car, and so he just shrugged and disappeared back into the kitchen.

"David, are you OK? I know you have had to deal with some really strange stuff lately, but is everything OK with you? Sorry about Roger." Becky's warm, soft voice and her soft hand on his arm brought David back to a mental happy place.

"Becky, I have been forced to do a lot of thinking about things, soul searching, I guess is what our parents might call it. I know this will sound a bit strange, but please let me ramble for a minute or two so that I can hear myself say it. I'm not sure I will even like what I hear. Becky, I think I know what I have to do. I think all these crazy visions and stuff that have been happening are starting to coalesce into a direction for me. I guess I don't really know if this is what I'm supposed to do, but it feels like what I have to do." David continued to talk about his feelings in ways that Becky would only expect from one of her girlfriends, not from her big, strong Idaho farm boy. "I need to reach out to people that are not as fortunate as me. You see, I think the car is emblematic of this situation. I think the Saint Joseph guy had to come and push me to refocus my attention in this direction. Heck, I guess he probably knew I was getting the car for Christmas, right? Maybe he was like 'Bel Air' man all along."

"David, what makes you think that these episodes are tied to some kind of enlightenment or calling? It seems to me that you are reading more into this than the evidence would allow." Becky could not help but let her skepticism slide through in her voice.

"Becky, think about it. This can't just be random hallucinations. I mean, why would I be even seeing this Saint Joseph guy at all unless there was some reason to it?" David seemed to be trying to convince himself as much as Becky. "I don't really have any kind of scientific evidence like we would need in Mr. Hartley's physics class, but in my gut I really feel like this whole situation might be starting to make some sense and might be leading me somewhere."

Becky studied his face as David spoke. "Ok, now I'm really starting to wonder. Where do you think this is leading you? Wait, before you answer that one, how can you be sure this isn't just bizarre hallucinations that don't really mean anything? Honestly, David, you don't even sound like yourself!"

"Maybe this is the me that has always been inside but covered with the veneer of a cynical world's material values? I know that I can't just ignore what has happened, or pretend that I didn't even experience anything. I have an opportunity to do something about people's lives that I didn't even know existed until this strange man showed up in my life. He opened my eyes to the world right in front of me here in Seltice Falls, while all the time I had been focused on the world outside of this place."

David's voice carried an emergent passion that Becky had not witnessed previously, even when he spoke of watching the Mercury program at the new NASA space agency, a topic that David was very passionate about.

David's enthusiasm continued. "It's like this car. Two weeks ago, I would have reveled in having this car, cruising around town and showing it off to all of my friends, but now it almost feels like a burden. I know how bizarre that must sound, Becky, but all I can say is that is how I'm feeling about it."

Becky felt like she was sitting next to a stranger as David spoke. His words and explanations did not fit the young man she thought she knew. She felt herself mentally scooting away from him on the sofa. "Ok, David, for argument's sake, let's say you're right. Heck, let's say that this was Saint Joseph coming down from above to visit you with a message. Visit little old David Edmonds in tiny Seltice Falls, Idaho. So what? I mean, what can you do about other people's lives anyway? Most people make choices in life that result in consequences, so you can't always help people the way that you think."

"OK, be cynical if you want, but I know what I know about this and it wasn't just some conjured-up dream that I had late at night. Heck, you saw evidence yourself. Besides, some people don't have any choice, like Johnny Bates in his situation of a broken home and meager resources, it's not like those were his choices. I can do something. Heck, I could sell the car and use the money to help people who didn't have such a nice Christmas. Yes, yes, I could use the money from the car to help people." David's eyes widen as he envisioned his idea.

"What! Sell the car? You are going nuts, David. That was a gift from your parents. Selling the car would be like a slap in the face to them. I can't believe you are even thinking it, much less saying it!" Becky stood up as she spoke, no longer wanting to sit next to this sudden stranger in her living room. She marched toward the opposite side of the room, not really going anywhere, but needing to distance herself from David, at least for the moment.

David decided to sit silently as he watched Becky move away from him. Her body language was clear enough; she was not at all comfortable with this conversation. Improbably, he found that his desire for Becky was even stronger than usual when she was upset. Her own passions came through in a way that made David want to jump from the sofa and put his arms around her. He wanted to smell her sweet aroma and feel the soft touch of her lips and the gentleness of their bodies embracing. In spite of his impassioned imagination, he did not dare move from the sofa. He knew Becky well enough to know that such an attempt would not be welcomed when she was upset with him. He was frustrated with his inability to convey his revelations about his visitations to Becky in such a way as to convince her to see the truth in his newfound view of the world.

Becky spoke without facing David. She spoke in a forceful, almost mocking tone that made David feel like he was a stranger to her. "David, I don't mean to dismiss your experiences or your interpretations of them. Obviously, they are well intended, but it just seems like you are putting too much credibility into them when you draw these conclusions. I see my boyfriend talking in a way that I don't even recognize. Can't we just be high school sweethearts without all this drama of an imagined old man and your life changes as a result? Ok, sorry, maybe not an imagined old man, but possibly, what, Saint Joseph? David, it sounds crazy when it comes from my mouth!"

David sat silently as he watched Becky. He found himself admiring her petite body, her soft, rich hair, and the way she stood away from him. He did not really have any answers for her. He knew that if he was in her position, he would probably take an even more skeptical view of things, and he couldn't blame her for such doubt. He knew that if he had discussed this with anyone else, outside of Father Donovan, they would probably have sent him to the psyche ward for help. Probably even Father Donovan thought he was nuts but couldn't say anything outside the confessional.

Unlike most of their time together, there was now a tension in the room between them. This was foreign to them and they didn't really know how to process their emotions toward each other. The silence that had settled was engulfing them. David quelled his emotional desires for Becky and continued to sit quietly on the sofa. Becky stood and stared at the fireplace, keeping her back to David. She did not know how to defuse the tension that stretched between them. David continued to sit dolefully on the sofa and mull his inner mental storm, while he watched Becky's back.

Mary Marston noticed the sudden quiet from her place in the kitchen where she was wrapping up chores from the Christmas holidays. She stepped out to see what was happening and immediately understood that her daughter and David were having a tiff. She wisely backed away and let the young sweethearts work out things for themselves. In doing so she had to suppress a bit of a smile as she thought back to her own romance and relationship with her husband and the times they had quarreled, quarrels that now seemed minor and agonizingly hollow.

David finally rose from the couch and approached Becky. He stepped behind her and touched her lightly on her arms. As he did, he could feel her muscles tense and knew that she was not ready to embrace him. Being a sensitive person, David only wanted to make Becky feel comfortable. "Becky, I know that I've upset you with all of this stuff and that it's all been very sudden. You know, though, that I have always tried to be nothing but honest with you, and that is why I have shared my inner feelings regarding my experiences. I hope you can understand that and at least accept my sincerity."

Becky relaxed and turned to David, letting his hands grip her arms and stepping toward his embrace. "Oh, David, you know how I feel about you, and I want the best for you, but this, this crazy stuff is just too much to grasp in such a short time. I may just need some time to catch up with where you are in your analysis of events."

They both relaxed and embraced, but it was evident that something had changed between them. The embrace seemed more platonic than romantic. David knew it was time to leave. He gave Becky a light kiss and a final hug before he took his leave and headed back toward the waiting Chevy.

She stood on the old porch and stared at the door for several minutes, not sure if she should really knock. Becky felt both embarrassed and excited, and probably also fearful of what her emotions would do to her demeanor once that door opened, a door that might represent a past that she was not sure she should revisit. She closed her eyes and tried to steady herself, she was surprised to find that her emotions were that of a teenage girl waiting on a boy. Maybe it was only yesterday.

"Grandma, what are we doing? I'm cold. Aren't we going to go in?" The pleading voice of her shivering grandson brought her back to the present day.

"Yes, Tommy, of course we are going to go in. Nana just needs to think a minute." Becky brushed her grandson's soft brown hair as she thought about his life. His life in the future and the many twists and turns he will face, all of which are unknown to him, unknown to all. Becky felt like leaving might be the easier option, as she wasn't even sure what prompted her to drive to this parish today to see her old sweetheart.

She had put David Edmonds out of her mind for most of the past thirty years, but at Christmas season her heart would always spring with long-quiet emotions for her teenage heartthrob. It was even more acute if she encountered a restored 1955 Chevrolet Bel Air. Emotions she had forced herself to abandon many years ago would suddenly engulf her and find a way to moisten her eyes no matter how practiced she might be at containing her feelings. She stroked her grandson's hair and contemplated her situation, standing less than elegantly on the parsonage stoop. As she continued to look from the door to Tommy, her face started to relax and she felt a soft smile start to erupt as she thought about a long-ago Christmas and the life that followed, a good life but not the one she might have imagined back at Christmas 1962.

Becky squeezed her right hand into a tight fist and let it flex for several oscillations before seeing her hand raise up, as if of its own volition, and strike the door sharply. The knock rang out on the solid oak door with authority and more volume than she had anticipated. She looked curiously and momentarily at her clenched fist that had just invited the past to pierce into her world. She stepped back as her fear of this past, so long ago locked away in her heart, was possibly now coming to the door. She shuddered slightly as she thought about the wisdom of coming here today.

She could hear someone approach the door and watched as the tarnished brass knob obediently turned and the massive oak door swung inward to reveal a young priest with a smile as he studied his guests. "Good morning. May I help you?"

"Good morning, Reverend, I mean, Father." Becky tried to calibrate to the Catholic custom of addressing priests. "Yes, we are here to see David Edmonds. Is he here?"

"You mean Father Edmonds?" The puzzled priest rotated his gaze from woman to boy.

"Yes, yes, of course, I mean Father Edmonds, sorry." Becky chuckled a bit at this slip. "Sorry, old habit from long ago."

"No problem at all. Please come into the parlor and I will ring Father Edmonds. I believe he just returned from some local meetings." The priest waved his arm in the direction of the front room and toward a sofa.

Becky and Tommy sat on the sofa as the young priest dutifully left to find David. Becky's palms were sweating in spite of the cold weather they had just left on the front porch. She rubbed her hands together and once again silently questioned the wisdom of this visit. Her eyes took in the room and the sights of this place that David called home. A home far removed from their shared experiences in Seltice Falls. David had moved onto the larger city life of Seattle while Becky had eventually landed in Chicago. The room was pleasant enough, neat to a fault, with pleasant furnishings, impressive paintings of bible scenes, and a saintly statue thrown in for good measure. Her eyes came to rest on a particular statue of Saint Joseph. The statue was larger than the others and carried a peculiar coloring of garments. She smiled again as she knew this statue most certainly must be the personal property of David. Although the house was lived in, it did not give that sensation. The obvious lack of any children living here gave the building an almost institutional feel, not quite sterile but more like an elderly person's home.

Her observations of the room had distracted her enough that she did not notice David bound into the room.

"Becky! Oh my gosh, Becky!" David's mouth broke into such a broad, happy smile that it seemed to split across his entire face.

"David!" Becky's concern about visiting rapidly dissipated into the suddenly warm ambiance of the room. Becky jumped from the sofa and crossed the room to meet David in his approach. They embraced in the middle of the room as Tommy watched, completely mystified as his grandma hugged this strange priest.

They hugged for a long moment. Becky's heart jumped with the resurgence of long-forgotten longings for this man, longings that she thought had eroded over the years since that strange Christmas so long ago.

"You should have let me know you were coming, I would have made sure there were some refreshments or something." David fumbled as he tried to strike the proper balance of conversation with his long-ago sweetheart.

"Don't be silly, David. Oh gosh, sorry, is it Father now?" Becky stepped back toward the sofa again.

"It's David to you. Hey, I think you are still Presbyterian anyway, right?" David laughed. "It's been too long, Becky."

"I know, David. I guess I haven't been very good at staying in touch. It seems life intervenes." Becky made her way back to the sofa.

"Yes, life has its own ideas sometimes, and I have not been the poster child of communication here either!" David took a seat on a nearby chair. "Who is this fine lad?" he continued while pointing toward Tommy.

Becky introduced a shy and annoyed Tommy, who looked at his shoes and tried to pretend not to care for this guy who had hugged his grandma.

They continued with small talk of families, shared memories, and catching up after almost thirty years of separation. Then Becky's tone transitioned to a more serious one. "The truth of it is, David, I never really could completely understand your faith in what happened that Christmas. You were the stronger one in your faith and you acted on it. Whether or not you had personal visits with Saint Joseph, well, who knows, but regardless, you followed your heart. Who can criticize you for that?"

David let this settle in for a few seconds. "I can't deny that it changed my life in ways that I could have never even imagined. I never even considered being a priest before that Christmas. I feel like maybe I cheated in some ways."

Becky's seemed puzzled by this remark. "Cheated? What in the world are you talking about? I have followed your career as a cleric and I know how much you have accomplished for the poor and underprivileged. The world would have been cheated if you had taken a different road in life."

David smiled, as he knew what she meant by a different road. "What I mean is that I don't know any other people who sacrifice and dedicate themselves to the ministry who had the privilege of a personal visit from a saint. Why did this happen to me? I can only conclude it was God's plan and let it go at that, but I always have this gnawing feeling that more is expected of me because of my experience."

"Well, I think you have done everything that could have been expected of you, and then some." Becky looked David in the eye as she concluded.

David smiled again. "I appreciate that very much, Becky, and you know I'm really glad that you were there to share that with me. Honestly, I don't know what I would have done if I would have had to deal with it all on my own. Well, there was Father Donovan, but honestly he was not that helpful."

"Father Donovan? Did he know about the Saint Joseph thing?" Becky's eyebrows raised, as this was completely new information.

"Yes, I probably never mentioned it, but I did confess my experience to him in the confessional. I think he probably thought I was nuts. Can't say that I blame him, though." David watched Tommy as he spoke.

Becky transitioned the conversation. "I can still remember how absolutely *nuts* everyone thought you were when you sold that beautiful 1955 Chevy and used the money to help Johnny Bates get a college application and scholarships. I think your parents probably about killed you, too."

David laughed aloud. "My dad was livid, at least at first. I guess I can understand that since he worked hard to give his son such an amazing gift and then to have his son give it away would be upsetting. My mom was actually pretty cool about it. I think she saw the big picture of my actions and appreciated it for that. Of course, all of that changed things between you and me. I was never really happy about that. You know I felt strongly about you."

Becky wanted to shout at him, "Of course I know, you idiot. I was in love with you!" But instead she nodded. "I had strong feelings for you, too, David, but I just did not understand what was going on with you and your change to this godly person. And when you said you were going to leave Seltice Falls to enter the seminary, well, I knew that was it for me."

"Yes, I guess it must have seemed really strange at the time." David nodded.

"Pretty strange! It was off the charts ridiculous. I mean, even your folks, who were strong Catholics, were dismayed at your sudden change in personality, behavior, and everything. You don't know how traumatic it was for me, for all of us." Becky did not realize that these emotions about David from thirty years before were still harboring within her soul, and she now felt a little embarrassed as they erupted out without her consent. She tried to recover a bit. "Sorry, David, I don't know where that came from. I think seeing you again opened an old wound that I did not even know was still festering. After all, it was your life, and what a great life you have made it."

"Becky, please. Believe me, I understand. Oh, I didn't back then. I was a selfish teenager with a newfound enlightenment that I had to act upon. I did it without really considering the consequences or impacts to others, people I loved and cared about. My parents, siblings, friends, and, of course, you, Becky. I'm not saying I regret taking this priestly path, but my methodology left a lot of wreckage in its wake. I hope you can understand, and if it makes any difference, I am sorry for any pain that my selfish behavior may have caused you." David rose and took Becky's hand. Although her hand wore the creases and lines of thirty years of being a wife, mother, and career executive, they still had that magical sensation to David's touch.

Becky could feel the warmth of her 1962 high school sweetheart in David's hands, which were still youthful looking in spite of the years, and still looked familiar. They were hands that she still cared for, even though the logical part of her mind tried to say otherwise. Becky tried to hold back the tears welling up in her eyes, but she knew already that she would lose this battle, and now she wondered about the wisdom of even coming here today. Why had she come, and what did she expect to find. She already knew in her heart that she expected to find her David, and unfortunately for her, that is exactly what she found.

Becky stood and embraced David as she wept, her soft face on his shoulder and her tears dampening his black clergy jacket. Their embrace was oddly familiar, even if such sensations had lain dormant for decades. David was amazed that he could recognize the same sweet scent on Becky's neck, a smell that took him back to times on the Marston couch, hugs in the darkened interior of a long-ago

Buick, and their unplanned encounters in the halls of Seltice Falls High School.

After an emotional moment, David gripped Becky's arms and stepped back to gaze into her watery eyes. "I'm glad you stopped by. I doubt that you get to Seattle very often, as I know how busy you must be as a mom and grandmother, as well as a wife and executive. Your husband and extended family are very blessed to have you in their lives. We had a wonderful, youthful relationship, and for that we should be grateful, but of course that is in the past, where it must remain."

Becky nodded and smiled. "Yes, sorry. I did not realize how emotional it would be to see you again, David. You are right. I am very blessed with my family and life. God has been good to me."

They held each other's gaze for a moment longer and then quietly returned to their respective seating positions and resumed their conversation.

"Did you ever regret your decisions or actions, David? Sorry, I didn't mean it like that. I'm just curious since it was such a radical departure from the David we knew at the time." Even as she spoke, Becky felt that maybe she had embarked too far into now-private matters with this approach, especially to a man that she really hardly knew.

"No, it's fine, and yes, I think one always thinks back about the choices they make in life. That is really what life is about, isn't it, the choices we make? We all make good ones and bad ones. The objective is to learn from both and over time to get the balance beam to tip toward the good ones over the bad ones. I certainly don't regret the path into the priesthood, but I know I could have taken that divergence with less anguish than what I did. Such is youthful self-aggrandizing, thinking of oneself over others. Besides hurting my parents and you, I always felt bad about my friendship with Mike Glatter. Mike and I were best friends from almost first grade, but after that Christmas we drifted apart, mostly due to me and my newfound enlightenment. I was able to leverage my changes to help Johnny Bates, though, and that turned out to be a good decision. Did you know that with my financial help and emotional encouragement he ended up with a business degree from the University of Idaho and eventually an MBA from Wharton? I think he realized that he could grow a new branch on that family tree and make his own way. He still stays in touch with me and stops by to visit when he's in town for business. It's really amazing what faith, determination, good decisions, and God can do when you let them. I mean, look at you and how successful you are in life, and I don't mean the financial part, even though that is impressive. I mean the important part—love, family, faith, and the rest of it. You are a corporate executive in finance, a great mom, a grandmother, a wife, and I know you are good person. I have always known that about you." David's face broke into a broad smile as his eyes met Becky's.

Becky could not hold back her smile. "I appreciate your kind words about my life and decisions but, of course, all of that has tradeoffs, doesn't it? I have a good life, a comfortable life, but it has its cost. I didn't get to be the mom that my mom was to me. With travel, long hours, and busy schedules between my husband and me, we don't have the nice, simple family time that I enjoyed growing up in Seltice Falls. Don't get me wrong, I don't regret the path I took but, well, you know, it has its price."

"Of course, that is the same for all of us. I would have liked to have been a father and husband but that was not possible with my choice of the priesthood." David relaxed back in his sofa.

Becky shifted gears. "Did you have more of the visions? Sorry, just curious."

David smiled again. "Funny you should ask. For some reason, I didn't expect any more and as it turned out, there were no more. The last time was in the church when I was speaking to who I thought was Father Donovan, but as he was leaving the church I could see that it was Saint Joseph, not Father Donovan. I guess he knew that his mission was accomplished at that point."

Becky cocked her head toward David. "Mission? What was his mission then?"

"To me it was focusing my life toward the Lord and away from the material world. I guess that beautiful Chevy was a manifestation of my worldly desires. At least that is the way I concluded the overall experience and made my choices. I can only trust God that I did the right things." David's facial muscles had a sad air as he considered his thoughts aloud.

"I admire you that you were able to draw such a resilient conclusion about life at such an early age. Really, that is not something you would expect from a teenager. I was quite skeptical of your visions, even after the experience with the footprints in the snow, at least until you related your visit to my dad's funeral. That unnerved me. I knew from that point you were not just having some imaginary daydream but something more. In spite of my being convinced of the reality of your experiences, I did not want to compete with them, or Saint Joseph! Ah, but such is life, eh?" Becky met David's gaze, still with puppy love in her eyes but with the knowledge that this was as far as she could ever take her feelings.

"I'm sorry you felt you had to compete with them or him. I guess that was my fault. I will have to chalk that one up to being a selfish teenager. I guess God had different paths for both of us. I think he had a great path for you, Becky, and I can see it in this fine grandson of yours." David held her gaze as he spoke.

They continued to chat and catch up on life events and personal experiences. The conversation turned to more mundane topics and their feelings toward each other ebbed more toward that of old acquaintances than former sweethearts. Becky concluded the visit with her need to be on her way and back to her life as a finance director for a major insurance firm. They hugged once again and took one last gaze, through tear-filled eyes, as they parted toward their separate lives.

David, now Father Edmonds, stood on the stoop of the parish house and waved to Becky as she backed out onto the street and slowly drove away. David smiled as he noticed that Becky was driving a Buick, and he felt a long-forgotten pang for this girl who had once stolen his teenage heart. Clearly she still possessed a part of it. Becky watched David in the mirror for as long as safe driving would allow. She rounded the corner at the end of the block and then he was gone from view and once again from her life. As if on cue, the radio started to blare out Don McLean's "American Pie" anthem to lost youth.

Becky smiled and said aloud, "Ok, Saint Joseph, I hear you. Don't worry, your David is still with you."